Fen

Julie Ankerson

To my family, and John and Harriet

CHAPTER ONE

Fen wasn't surprised that the day was turning out this way. She knew she should have been suspicious when it started out so well. The alarm clock hadn't needed to wake her; she had beaten it to it. Her eyes weren't heavy and gummy, her hair wasn't silly and her back didn't hurt.

She had put on a rather jolly orange flowery shift dress, her lovely bargain patent leather shoes and strolled, light hearted, to catch the splendid, punctual, empty bus.

And now she was sitting in a swanky Art Deco leather and chrome chair in her agent's office, feeling all of the joy wheeze out of her.

Edgar "Eggy" Egremont looked at her with an expression of detached concern that she suspected he had probably been practising all morning in his bathroom mirror. His smooth face and his smooth hair reflected back up to him from the surface of his shiny black ash table.

"So, sweetie, you do understand?"

It wouldn't really matter to Eggy in the slightest if she didn't; she was only on his books because her brother had gone to school with his wife, the wife Eggy didn't like to talk about as she rather upset the façade of camp theatricality he affected to assume.

"Well, yes, from your point of view, I suppose..." Fen's voice sounded squeaky and sad and she wondered if she might cry.

He was right of course; she hadn't had much work recently. There had been a small walk on part in 'The Huntsman', a detective series. She had played a party girl who met a grisly end with a cocktail stick through the eye. Rather well, she thought, or, at least, with vigour and conviction.

"You just don't appear to be a popular type at the moment, honey." Eggy smiled tightly and looked a bit bored; he was thinking about his lunch appointment with a lovely young actress called Stella and fervently hoping Fen didn't make a scene.

'Ah,' thought Fen. 'So that's it, fat knees. I knew this would happen. My entire life ruined by fat knees, and fat hands. And the wrong hair.'

It was true; she didn't match the current trend of willowy, long haired, long legged lovelies who swooped easily from the catwalk, effortlessly making the transition onto film and television screens. Her hair was big and brown and curly, her nose a bit too snub and her knees a little too…fat.

'Character roles! I could be maids, nurses, old prostitutes!'

She was glad she didn't say it out loud, as it suddenly occurred to her that maybe the problem might not only be the bigness of her knees, but also the smallness of her talent.

Fen noticed that she had slumped into a small deflated puddle on the shiny chair and moved to straighten herself up, trying to unstick her bare legs from the leather without making an embarrassing squelching noise.

"Maybe I will see you at Justin's some time?" Eggy arched an elegant eyebrow and glanced at his expensive watch.

'Ten per cent of my money went to buy that,' thought Fen, and then remembered that ten per cent of what she had earned over the last year probably wouldn't even have paid for a hole in the strap.

"Yes, that would be fabulous!"

Her voice still sounded squeaky; that voice coach had been a waste of money too, and fabulous? No it wouldn't. Hearing Eggy name drop about his marvellous celebrity friends and the exquisite restaurants he visited, whilst her brother gazed at him with a befuddled air, wondering if he would leave soon so that he could get on with his painting, would be utterly dire.

"Thanks for everything, Eggy!"

Or nothing. As she left, Fen knew she had red marks on the back of her legs from the chair, knew she would pull the door when it should be pushed. In fact, she may as well just break wind and fall over for good measure. But somehow she was down the stairs and blinking in the thin sunlight on the London street, wondering where the hell she went from here.

Half past ten, should she just go back home? Great Marlborough Street seemed strangely quiet, everyone busy at work.

'Work,' thought Fen. 'A job. I don't have one'.

The street was cold despite the April sunshine, the buildings cast long shadows and she wished she had worn a coat. She felt surreal, inert, all the things she would have liked to have said to Eggy now racing round her head. If he had been a better agent, if he had introduced her to the right people, given her more support. Then childish insults started to crowd her mind and the desire to march back up to his office and push a pie in his face. But she didn't have a pie, or the money to waste on a pie she couldn't eat.

Fen remembered, though, that she had just received a royalty payment for a television series she had been in three years ago, playing the daughter of a country vet. Happy times; twelve weeks in Gloucestershire; such laughs every night back at the big house. And Tommy had been there. She shook herself mentally. No point thinking about that now. Anyway, her character had met a terrible end off screen on the horns of a bull. She'd been given a lovely funeral, but the series went on successfully without her.

The money would just about cover three months rent on her flat in Tottenham, or, a little devil popped up on her shoulder, she could go to Liberty's and buy some lovely shiny jewellery to cheer herself up. Fen started to walk towards Argyll Street, trying to make a plan. The desire to just go home and lock the door, sit in a corner with a bag over her head and do some rocking was quite strong, but maybe, she thought, it might be more productive to go up Oxford Street to Selfridges and ask for work. She had worked there one Christmas and had enjoyed it, so that wouldn't be so bad. Or she could get herself another agent, someone young and enthusiastic and not so interested in dinners and dolly birds. But could she keep putting herself through this? Fen was thirty two now, Hollywood was not going to happen and her knees were still too fat for today's tastes.

'Maybe an extensive knee exercise regime, a specific knee diet.'

She realised she was going a bit weird and faint, probably needed a cup of tea and something nice and cheesy to eat. She turned back on herself to go to her favourite café, the Acropolis, but the lovely patent leather bargain shoes no longer made her feel optimistic and had started to rub her heels. It dawned on her that the pub would be opening soon and was nearer than the café. Alcohol seemed suddenly appealing.

'Plus,' Fen thought, 'I might bump into someone I know, someone with a sudden exciting job vacancy, ha ha.'

She wondered if her friend Maisie might be in the Ann Boleyn in Dean Street. Maisie worked at one of the many post-production houses around Soho as a receptionist. She had taken the job as a means to bagging a film star husband, but had ended up with Jim, the projectionist's assistant, instead. Jim was sweet and kind and bald and dull and Maisie loved him really.

The pub door opened onto a comforting nicotine fug and Fen spotted a chair in the corner, warmed in a pool of sunlight, that looked as if it could be a nice home for a few hours.

The pub wasn't very busy yet, its only inhabitants a tweed jacketed man talking to a thin, elderly, mad haired woman, and a couple of young men from a nearby construction site. They only glanced at Fen as she approached the bar, which both relieved and depressed her.

"Campari and orange," she told the barman, thinking the frivolity might cheer her up, and she made her way to the sanctuary of the sunlit chair.

The bitterness of the drink perked her up slightly and she watched the dust motes and the cigarette smoke dance through the air. She wondered if she might like a Scotch egg or a sandwich. Then, for a while, she thought of nothing at all and just stared into space.

Her first drink had nearly gone and the pub was beginning to fill up. Fen started to worry that a stranger might want to share her table or, worse still, a conversation with her. And there was also the added danger that, if she went to the bar for another drink, someone might steal her seat. She stared at the pub door, willing a friendly face to appear. She also might need the Ladies, so a decision would have to be made soon. And then, to her great relief, Maisie's bright bottle blonde head popped into view as she scuttled in, nagging behind her to Jim.

"FENELLA ROMAINE, you absolute BITCH!!" screeched Maisie, causing a small pause in the drinking of many lunch time pints.

"Maisie Peters, you dirty old besom." Fen's reply was far quieter, which was odd, considering which one was meant to be the actress. As Maisie hugged her in a cloud of Miss Dior, and their bosoms squished together, a little sad thought reminded Fen that her knees weren't the only thing too big for today's tastes.

"What are you doing here, you tart? You never write, you never phone. JIM, get us some drinks. You still drinking that nasty concoction?" Maisie made herself comfortable, shedding bags and scarves and gloves, even though she had only walked from two doors down the street. Jim looked a bit glum.

"Do I really have to ask for that? They always look at me funny."

"You get Fen her dirty drink and shut up. So how are you, you old cow, how's Justin and the girls, Sandy, your mum and dad?"

Her poor old mum and dad. They were so secretly proud of their daughter, especially when she had been in 'We Live On The Farm'. Oh well. They did keep telling her to get a proper job (now they had given up on 'when are you going to get married?').

"Fine, all fine. You still with your young man then?"

Fen nodded towards Jim, who was making a very bad job of getting served at the bar, as if he had struck himself invisible.

"Yeah, bless him. Bores me stupid, but he'll do for now. How 'bout you? What you working on?"

Fen took a little breath in.

"Aah, now there's a thing. That bloody Eggy git Egremont has just informed me I'm not on his books any more and he won't be bothering to send me to castings".

Fen wished Maisie looked a little more surprised.

"But you know so much about all his shenanigans. You should see him up our place, pretending to be gay and luring all those silly girls with promises of work. Can't you get Justin to tell his wife? Blackmail him into taking you back?"

Fen had to admit it had crossed her mind when she was feeling particularly evil. "Nah," she replied. "It would feel too mean. Sonia's lovely and Justin would never remember if I told him. He's got an exhibition coming up and he can't think of anything else."

Jim was making his way over and had only spilt a bit of Campari down his arm. He plonked the drinks down and looked round for a spare chair.

"JIM!" snapped Maisie. "Can't you find someone else to talk to? Look - Harry from Transfer Bay is at the bar. Go and talk to him about the Arsenal or something."

"But I..." Jim realised he would inevitably be beaten and gave up trying to finish the sentence, picked up his pint and shuffled off. Maisie sneered at his back.

"Look at that God awful jumper. His Mum knitted it, I ask you. We're getting married in June."

"Is that good?" laughed Fen.

Maisie tapped her arm. "Cheeky. You must come. I like your dress."

Fen thanked her and showed off her bargain shoes and they had a little chat about such things. Then Maisie asked, "So what are you going to do for money?"

Fen pursed her lips and swirled her drink around the glass, distracted by its orangey pinkness.

"I have no idea. Shop work? Secretarial? Astronaut?".

"Could those busters defy gravity?" teased Maisie.

"Slut, yours are miles bigger. I just don't know, Maisie. I liked being an actress. I like the showing off, the camaraderie."

"The rejection, the backstabbing, the never knowing if you can pay the rent." Maisie looked at her with concern. "Seriously though, Fen, you meet people, say you'll be friends forever. Then, when the play's over or the film's wrapped, you never see them again, except perhaps when you're up for the same job and you can 'Darling, Darling!!' each other through gritted teeth. Wouldn't you like to settle down, have some stability?"

They both looked over at Jim, who was staring at the dartboard with his mouth open, and Fen realised that she didn't actually feel all that thrilled at the prospect.

She sighed and sank back into her chair with a small plaintive creak.

"I know what you mean, but there must be something I can do that's not utterly dull."

Maisie looked at her with pity. "Look, soppy, all jobs are dull. I bet even being an astronaut can seem pretty dull after a while, all that pissing in your suit. If you were still in 'We Live On The Farm', you would be sick to death by now of saying 'Father, I'm off to move the bullocks'."

Fen laughed, but looked mulish. "Oh, boo to it all. When do you have to go back to work?"

Maisie glanced at her watch. "Too soon, my sweet, too soon. We've got a load of bit part actors, oops, no offence, coming in to do dialogue loops for that cheapo spy film, 'The Man With The Iron Leg', this afternoon and I'll have to send them to the right place."

Fen felt even glummer. "I auditioned for that. Sadie Loveword, assistant to the villain. Apparently I was the wrong shape."

Maisie laughed, but not unkindly. "Jim's seen most of it. Despite the beautiful women, even he thinks it's dire. I think Stella Jensen got your part."

Fen filled her mouth with the ice from the bottom of her glass and snorted. "Eggyth new squeeth."

Maisie patted her hand sympathetically, and shrieked, "JIM!! MORE DRINKS," and pulled a sad face at Fen. "I've just remembered. The sound editor on the film also worked on 'We Live On The Farm', nice old boy, Geoff Lewis. Did you meet him?"

Fen dragged her mind back. She had been so scared of doing dialogue replacement, recreating a performance in a cold clinical studio weeks later when you had quite forgotten any motivation you ever had, that the other people present became a bit of a threatening blur. Plus, she had still been so depressed about her character's rapid departure. That time had been saved by meeting Maisie; she had calmed her nerves slightly with a big, secret cup of gin.

"Geoff, Geoff...glasses? Grey hair? That look of having been locked away for years somewhere dusty and dark?"

Maisie smiled. "Well, that last bit describes all of them, but yes. Here's my boy!" Jim slid their drinks onto the table and sidled off.

Fen took a sip and started to feel on the tipsy side; too late for the Scotch egg now. "Yes I do remember him. His son was a runner on location."

Maisie finished her drink in one big go and started to gather up her belongings. "Come back and say hello. You can't stay in here on your own. Sit out the back with Jim and laugh at Stella's performance. You know you want to."

Fen dithered. What she really wanted was five more drinks, a big dinner and a bigger cry.

"Oh go on then," and she followed Maisie, who had grabbed Jim by the arm, out onto Dean Street.

CHAPTER TWO

As they all burst into the main reception of Huntley Post-Production Studios, Fen caught sight of herself in the big mirror. Her face was pink and her brown eyes were glittery and squinty. 'I look tiddly,' she thought. Her earlier, forgotten need for the Ladies had returned with great urgency and she leapt into the lift after Jim, miming her intention at Maisie, who waved and blew her a kiss.

Also, she didn't want to risk bumping into Stella, and Eggy might be with her. She shuddered, goose bumps rising on her bare arms; she'd had enough of that man for today.

Jim was waiting patiently for her outside the toilets when Fen emerged, looking slightly more composed, and she followed him up the stairs to the projection booth.

Len, the chief projectionist, had also been in the pub that lunchtime. He had been in the pub every lunchtime for the past thirty five years, and it showed in the crazy patchwork of veins on his red face. He was very, very drunk and was ineffectually trying to prise the lid from a metal film can. Jim, with the resigned air of someone who knew he was carrying on an ancient tradition, and that in about 10 years another younger man would be doing the same for him, gently pushed Len into a chair, gave him a copy of the Sun and expertly opened the can.

While Jim laced up the projector and got the loops ready for the afternoon session, Fen found a dusty, green, metal legged chair with a pile of porn mags stacked on top. Grimacing, as in her mind she imagined them sticky to the touch, she prodded them off gingerly with a nearby chinagraph pencil. Dragging the stool from under one of the viewing windows, she settled herself down and peered down into the dimly lit studio below.

She gave a little squeak of joy when the first artist came in. It was Petie. She had worked on an episode of 'Grainger' with him. 'Grainger' was a popular series about an alcoholic policeman working in Gibraltar. Sadly, the scenes Fen and Petie were involved in had been recorded in Hayes on a very wet Tuesday afternoon. Petie had played a gun runner and Fen had been his cuckolded wife who had 'grassed him up' to Grainger, and she had had so much fun filming it. Petie was magnificent. His mother was from Sweden and his father was from Trinidad. Six foot two of pure muscle with a chiselled jaw, he was always cast as villains. In reality, he was as soft as whipped cream and a devil with the boys.

Fen gazed at the back of Petie's beautiful head and lost herself in his velvety warm tone as he started to re-voice the loops for the film. Jim laced up the magnetic tape loops onto the bays, ran the film on the projector and Petie would have to wait for the cue line, drawn onto the print with chinagraph pencil, and then try to synchronise his voice with the on-screen image.

A lot of actors hated this process, couldn't understand why they were being made to do it, and found it hard to get back into a character that they may have left behind them months ago. But it was necessary, sometimes to improve on a performance, but mostly to get a clean track free of background noise. Fen remembered tales of a Dickens adaptation that had filmed entirely on location near to the M1. So much of the dialogue had to be re-recorded that the actors may as well have just initially done the whole thing as a mime.

Petie was very good at the process, and was being incredibly patient with the young director, who, Fen would swear, was moments away from asking him to make his performance more 'purple'.

When the studio lights went up, Fen saw Geoff Lewis start sorting though a pile of papers while Petie thanked the sound engineer and kissed the director. She sprinted down the projection booth stairs (trying to ignore the niggling pain from her bargain shoes) to see if she could catch Petie on his way out. A hug from Petie was worth enduring any amount of pain; in fact, a run over hot coals would be perfectly acceptable for the pleasure.

"Petie!!" She caught up with him in the corridor by the lift. His face lit up as he turned and he swept her up and crushed her in a hug. He smelt delicious, a mix of tobacco flowers and sugar mice. Fen felt that pang of loss that all women felt with Petie, knowing they could never have him.

"Hello my lovely, who have you been up to?" he asked and kissed her full on the lips. If Fen had been in possession of a fan she would have hidden behind it and fluttered her eyelashes coquettishly. She wasn't though, so she giggled like a twelve year old and went a bit hot.

"Petie, you look fabulous, how are you? Are you busy?"

Fen realised she was gushing and maybe holding his hand a bit too tight, so she took a step back and knocked a framed photograph of David Niven sideways.

"Darling! Mind your poor head!" Petie reached behind her and straightened the picture. "I am fabulous, you must know that. And you, all jazzy in that splendid dress and those shoes! Divine."

Fen hoped he couldn't see the blood seeping down the side of them. She was suffering for this footwear perfection.

"And those lovely curls!" he went on. "You look like a woodland creature, like something from Narnia!"

Fen pulled a face. "You mean Mr. Tumnus?"

"Well darling, now you mention it, you might shave your legs more often."

Fen slapped him on the arm, desperately wishing she could rub her legs to see if he was joking or not.

"Did you enjoy making the film?"

Petie raised his eyebrows. "Enjoy, enjoy? Well, I enjoyed the holiday in Morocco it paid for. Honestly sweetie, all I was there for was to look menacing in doorways. I swear I was just a massive draught excluder."

Fen giggled girlishly again. "What's next for you?"

Petie looked rather pleased. "A gladiator film, can you imagine? Oh the joy, I'll be oiled, rippling, everything."

The lift button lit red and Petie turned towards the door. "I think it's Stella coming in next, so I'll put my insincere 'love you darling' face on now. Don't be too devastated, you know you're my number one girl."

Fen was one hundred percent certain that this was indeed untrue, but enjoyed believing it for a moment. She wondered if she had time to run back to the booth before Stella emerged, all thin and young, but decided not to chance it in case a terrible tripping over her own feet, sprawling face down on the floor incident occurred.

Stella stepped out of the lift, five foot ten, slender as a reed. She had a watery translucence, a siren, shipwrecking all the casting directors on her rock. Fen had never felt squatter, more dumpy, such a pudding. The sprawling on the floor incident might have been a chance worth taking after all.

"My beautiful." Petie winked at Fen as he wrapped himself around Stella, who winced a little at the force of his embrace. 'She is a fragile thing with her tiny bird like bones,' thought Fen. 'Hope he snaps her.'

Stella and Petie chatted about the people they'd met on the shoot for a while, and then Petie announced: "I'm off round the corner, see if I can't rustle up a little afternoon delight. Fen, have you met Stella?"

Shaking hands with her was like holding a dog biscuit and Fen wished she had touched the porn mags after all.

Stella's cool green eyes were looking over Fen's head at David Niven.

"Charmed," she whispered. "Likewise," replied Fen.

Petie waved as he stepped into the lift and Fen called out after him: "Be careful not to get your photo taken!" and he was gone and had taken all the air with him. Luckily, after an uncomfortable few seconds that went on for a year, with Stella gazing over Fen's head at her own reflection in the glass of David Niven's picture, the director came out of the studio and Stella was hustled in to go through her lines.

Fen wandered listlessly back into the projection booth. Jim was doing the job of two men whilst Len snored loudly in the corner. Fen had a passing urge to draw a moustache on him with magic marker as he slept, but was sure it had happened to him often before, so, not wishing to be repetitive, she took her place again on the metal stool. Stella seemed to have a great many dialogue lines to replace. Her beauty on screen was mesmerising, and, Fen grudgingly admitted to herself, she was a million times better in the part than Fen could have ever hoped to be. However, with her small breathy voice, the sound engineer was going through agonies trying to get enough level. Protocol being that he had to relay all his instructions to Stella through the director, he was running out of ways to ask diplomatically: "Could Miss Jensen try it a little louder?" "Could Miss Jensen project a little more on that line?" "Could Miss Jensen try again with a little more volume?" Fen stared at the top of his wispy head, willing it to explode so she could see the unsaid words, "FOR GOD'S SAKE, YOU SILLY COW, SPEAK LOUDER!!!!" burst out on springs and fly across the studio.

Eventually, she tired of trying to send soothing vibrations through the glass to un-tense the poor man's shoulders and realised that the long ago lunch time drinks had left an icky taste in her mouth. She looked at Jim, patiently pressing the rewind button on the projector.

"Jim?"

He turned, startled. "Blimey, you're so quiet, I forgot you were there! Not something I can ever say 'bout Maisie."

Fen smiled. "Is the tea bar open yet?"

Jim looked at his watch. "Yeah, she should be opening now."

Fen slid off the stool. "Two sugars?" She pointed at Len. "Should I...?"

"Nah," Jim replied. "He won't wake up 'til the pub's open again. Thanks love." He started rooting around in the pocket of his slacks for change, but Fen waved away the offer and set off, wondering if she could remember from her last visit where the tea bar was.

She found it eventually after a few dead ends, a couple of broom cupboards and nearly bursting into a live recording of 'Sing for your Life'. She remembered Frances, the elderly tea lady. Frances was hard to forget, with her tram-tracked, wrinkled face, jaunty wig and roll-up permanently on the go.

Frances herself had seen so many people in her thirty year service to refreshments that she had given up remembering anyone. All men were called Phil and all women were called Liz; Frances was a bit of a royalist on the quiet. "'Ello Liz love, what can I get you?"

"Two milky teas, please Frances, and two pieces of Victoria sponge."

Fen didn't like the look of the cake much. It appeared to have been sweating under its glass dome for a long time, but she was starved.

"Righty ho, Liz. Oh look, here's that Phil".

Fen glanced behind her and smiled as Geoff Lewis bumbled in. "Hello Geoff, I'm not sure if you remember me."

Geoff peered at her over his glasses. "It's Fen isn't it? You worked with my Ben."

"That's right. How is he getting on, been promoted yet?"

Geoff snorted. "He'll have to wait for a lot of men to die before he gets to wear their shoes. But he helps me out sometimes. He always talks kindly of you, you were sweet to him."

Fen blushed. "Aw, he was a lovely lad and it was a fun series to do. I had the time of my life..."

Seeing how wistful Fen looked, Geoff patted her shoulder.

"Yes, so sorry about your character's bull accident. Your send off was nice, though. Didn't they ask you to be the corpse?"

Fen laughed ruefully. "Yes they did, Geoff, but unfortunately my twitchy eye gave the game away, so my dead acting has been lost to the nation. Is Ben helping you out now?"

Geoff sighed. "I could do with him, but he's the runner on a sports quiz at the minute. This production's a nightmare. They've spent all the audio post budget on parties for the stars, so there's just two of us trying to sort out all the sound and it mixes in three weeks and now one of the footsteps artists has gone mad. Tea please Frances."

Fen's drinks were going cold and she wanted to eat her cake, but she liked Geoff, and his son reminded her of happier times, so she waited for him to be served and then accompanied him back to the studio.

"What are you working on at the moment then, Fen?" asked Geoff, following behind her in the corridor and carrying Jim's piece of cake.

"Nothing. My career seems to have gone up a dead end. Not sure if I'm going to carry on, to be honest. Might be time for a change."

Saying the words out loud scared Fen, but Geoff had perked up. "So you're free at the moment?"

Fen turned round and nodded. "Can you dance?" he asked her.

Fen was bemused; she had been in the chorus of a pantomime in Cardiff one year and had managed to sway in time with the music without drawing too much attention to herself

"Sort of…" she replied hesitantly.

"What are you doing this afternoon?" Fen knew she should really go home. Maisie and Jim would be going back to the Ann Boleyn as soon as work was over, probably staying until closing time, and she was a bit worried about getting so drunk with them that she ended up crying and being sick.

"Well .."

Geoff interrupted her. "Great. Just wait 'til whispering Stella's done her bit and I'll meet you in reception." He gave Jim's cake back to her and re-entered the studio. Fen wondered if she had just agreed to a life of exotic dancing in a back street club and took Jim his tea, now nearly stone cold with an unappetising film floating on the surface.

CHAPTER THREE

Fen ducked the hail of paper clips that Maisie threw at her, calmly saying, "You'll have to pick all those up now."

Maisie screwed up her clever pointy face. "Hee hee, I'll get Jim to do it. Have you finished ravishing my fiancé up the booth now?" Fen laughed and perched on the edge on Maisie's desk.

"I've just been keeping him hot for you. Actually, it would have been good practice. Geoff Lewis just asked me if I could dance and asked me to go somewhere with him. He's going to try and sell me for sex."

Maisie resolutely ignored the ringing phone. "You wouldn't get your bus fare home. I didn't have Geoff down as a randy old goat. Are you going to go?"

Fen thought for a bit. "Well I don't have much else on at the moment..."

"Damn you!" Maisie lunged at the receiver. "I'd better answer this. It is my job." She nodded towards the opening door.

"Here he is. Make sure you come to the pub to tell us what went on, if you're not in the hold of a ship bound for Fray Bentos. Good afternoon. Huntley Post-Production!!!"

'Such a lovely telephone manner,' thought Fen and smiled up at Geoff.

He had a pile of film cans under one arm and was trailing long paper cue sheets behind him from under the other. His glasses had slipped down to the end of his nose and he looked more grey faced and stressed than ever. Fen jumped up and took the papers from him, rolling them up into a tube. Geoff pushed his glasses back up and shifted the cans to get a better balance.

"Thank you dear. Off we go."

She opened the big glass door for him and followed as he sped scuttling off to the right. "It's just round here."

'Oh good, a back alley.' Fen really was having the strangest of days.

Geoff stopped in front of a battered green door and balanced the film cans so he could punch a code into a small metal keypad. There was a faint buzz and a click and he pushed through the door backwards. A pile of unclaimed post lay scattered by the side, and a flight of dimly lit stairs snaked down in front of them.

"Follow me. Not very plush I know, but their rates are cheap." Fen's mouth had gone very dry and she could only manage to bleat, "Oh."

Geoff paused outside a door covered in thick brown hessian and looked up at the red light above it.

'Please be a studio, not the other type of place with red lights,' prayed Fen. The light went off and Fen followed him in.

The dimly lit room was covered in the same brown material, the ceiling was very low and there was a strange dank smell of earth and old shoes. On the back wall, a projected image of Stella smiled seductively. Silhouetted against it, in front of a microphone, stood a tall, angry, middle aged woman.

"I demand you play it back. That one was fine. In fact, the first take was fine. I have been doing this for some time, you know."

She spotted Geoff. "Tell him, Geoff," she demanded peevishly.

Sitting behind a small mixing desk fiddling with a button, a blonde haired young man emanated exactly the same feelings as the engineer at Huntley Post. Again, Fen could almost see the unsaid words falling from his brain like ticker-tape.

Geoff dumped the cans on the floor. "Simon, turn the house lights on and get us some tea."

Simon the engineer sighed and flicked a switch, and a fluorescent light buzzed on. He pushed back his wheeled chair and stuck his hand out to Fen.

"Simon. Tea?" She shook it, smiling.

"Fen, yes please. Milk and one."

He mooched out, the door banging behind him. She tried to make sense of the room she was in; she had heard of this sort of thing going on behind the scenes, but had never really believed it. The studio seemed to be divided into rectangles with wooden edges on the floor, all containing different things: parquet in one, some concrete, gravel in another. Up against the wall leant the leg from a suit of armour. And on the left hand side, behind the tatty grey sofa where Geoff was trying to placate the angry lady, were four metal shelves just heaving with what could only be described as old tat.

A teapot, beads, dusty glasses, a bus ticket machine, a plastic monster's head, a cricket bat, a sword, piles of dusty cloth. Fen wondered if now might be a good time to run away. Next to the sofa was a large plastic container of water and a once-smart ladies' holdall spewing different shoes onto the floor. The lady sitting next to Geoff had her grubby trousers rolled up to mid-calf and was wearing odd socks, an oversized man's black punched leather brogue on the left foot and a sparkly silver stiletto heeled ladies' shoe, of giddying height, on the right.

She must have sensed Fen covertly trying to look her over, because a pair of small cold eyes sparked a glance at her.

Geoff introduced them. "Fen, this is Wanda Wender." The eyes narrowed and, with a tight wintry smile, Wanda said: "How nice," and carried on her tirade. She was an elegant woman, high cheekbones and powdery skin faintly etched with lines. Her hair was drawn back into a chignon, no stray hairs escaping; the crazy, smelly room seemed an unlikely place for her to be.

'There must be an empty sun lounger on a yacht in St. Tropez waiting for her. The crème de menthe will be getting warm,' Fen mused.

She hoped Simon would come back with the tea soon, or that Geoff would talk to her; she felt like a spare part leaning against the rough dirty wall.

Wanda seemed to have paused to take breath.

"So you don't think Miranda will be back tomorrow?" Geoff sounded defeated.

"She thinks it's a grubby little studio, and I agree. Where is the props man? The boom swinger? Who is that boy pulling me up on my sync? I hardly had an hour for lunch…"

"But you knew it was a low budget, Wanda. I managed to get both of you your daily rate and a two week schedule, but there just isn't the money to do it at Chivergreen."

Geoff glanced over at Fen, looking faintly surprised, as if he'd only just remembered she was there.

"Look, I've got you some help. If Miranda's determined she doesn't want to slum it, please, after all the jobs I've got for you, would you consider finishing the film for me? The director's insistent that he's got two more big budget films in the pipeline and we'll definitely be on them," he said.

Fen guessed that he was hoping Wanda might fall for 'my next film will be an epic'; She also suspected that he was well aware he was clutching at straws. An appeal to Wanda's vanity was probably the best way forward.

"No-one is as good as you and you know it. You've been carrying Miranda for years…" Fen saw the desperation in Geoff's eyes, waiting for the flattery to backfire. She could imagine the scene of the two women, bent over their cauldron,

Wanda hissing: 'and you will never guess what he said about you!!'

She did, however, seem to be relenting slightly.

"Help for me, you said. Shall I ring Luigi? He seemed to get on well last time," Wanda gambled, praying that Geoff didn't remember her boyfriend's creaky knee and his downright indolence.

"That is an idea, but we do need to get on quite urgently. Fen here..." He pointed over. "She used to dance. I'm sure she would love to have a go."

The studio was warm, and Fen had been feeling sleepy, but suddenly it was as if the doors had burst open, the roof had blown off and they were surrounded with snow, being eyed up by penguins.

"Have a go?" It was a whisper as chilly as a whistling North wind and Fen feared for her life.

"I could help....?" She wondered if anyone could hear her tiny scared voice. Wanda looked her up and down imperiously. "Are you a dancer?" This question seemed slightly more civil.

"I have danced." 'I am such a liar,' she thought.

"Who were you with?" Oh God, how far should she take this? Ballet Rambert? Bluebell Girls?

"A travelling show... Um. La Mère..." Damn it, what was the French word for Goose? "Canard". Oh, well done Fen, the Mother Duck travelling dance show. Time to go on the offensive.

"You must be a ballerina, with your beautiful poise. What productions might I have seen you in?"

Fen managed to get her voice back to an audible level and conjured up a winning smile. Wanda seemed to be thawing slightly.

"Yes I did train in 'The Ballet', but I am most well known for my television performances as the principal girl in Raymond Rumpole's Fondant Girls."

"Of course! I remember. You were an inspiration!" Fen wondered if she should carry on with her acting career after all; she seemed to be rather good at it at the moment. The Fondant Girls had been a regular turn on many variety and light entertainment shows, six beautiful girls wafting around in risqué outfits to popular tunes of the day.

Wanda got up. "We had better get started. There's only an hour left."

"Well, an hour and three quarters by my watch." Geoff resignedly glanced down at his wrist, and knew it would make no difference pointing this out.

"So you'll let Fen help?" Wanda gave an imperious nod. "Good, good. I'll tell Simon it's safe to come out now and we can get on."

Geoff went behind the control desk and flicked a switch. "Simon, you can make the teas now. Then we might manage a bit more before home time."

"So, how can I be most useful? I haven't a clue what's happening..." said Fen. Wanda had started sorting through her bag of shoes and looked up with a smile slightly warmer than any before. 'Spring is coming,' thought Fen.

"You could hand me things, dear, and move that microphone stand where Simon tells you to. That's not really our job and it's terribly heavy." 'Our job' sounded promising. Fen gratefully accepted a chipped mug of very brown lukewarm tea from Simon, who then settled himself back behind his console.

"Okay Wanda, once more from the top?"

Simon told Fen to position the microphone in front of the stone surface and lowered the house lights. He was a dry, dusty young man and the antagonism between him and Wanda was palpable. He seemed disappointed, as if he had been promised an exciting career in show business and had been left waiting for ten years in a cellar. Which, in truth, he had. He played the scene through with the guide sound for Wanda to watch. It was supposed to take place at night, but they had not yet darkened it in the grading, and you could hear a lively market nearby. Stella's character was rushing down an alley strewn with rubbish, dressed in a shimmering silver evening gown and looking behind her in fear.

Mid-way, Petie stepped out and grabbed her by the shoulders. According to the dialogue, he had been sent by the man with the iron leg to get her to inform on the whereabouts of her spy lover, if she knew what was good for her.

Simon rewound to the beginning, pressed 'play' and Wanda started to clip, clip in time with Stella using the foot with the stiletto on. The scene played again, and the process was repeated for Petie using the brogue. Simon then played the two together without the dialogue and background noise and the whole scene seemed suddenly more convincing.

The lights came back up. "Good," said Simon and started rustling through the long paper cue sheets. Fen thought it was better than good. Her estimation of Wanda rose; she thought it was very clever.

Geoff noticed her interest. "I'll be adding some city night atmospheres, you know, distant cars, a dog bark, that sort of thing, and then it will all be mixed together with the dialogue we were replacing over at Huntley Post this morning. I'll show you one day, if there's time. Simon, run the next cue."

After an hour, Wanda declared she needed 'washing up time' and went to make herself beautiful for the tube ride home. As she was leaving, she noticed Fen's poor bloodied heels from the bargain shoes.

"You poor dear, see if you can find yourself something else to wear home in my bag. You can bring them back tomorrow, and any other shoes you have that you think might sound good."

Geoff winked at Fen and mouthed, 'You've made a hit!'

Fen selected a pair of gold ballet pumps and, sighing with relief, followed him up the stairs, bidding good night to Simon as she went. Out in the street, Geoff shook her hand warmly.

"So you'll give it a go then?" Fen kissed him on the cheek. "I certainly will, and thank you so much for the chance. I'm really grateful."

Geoff shook his head. "Well, let's see if you're still thanking me and not killing me at the end of the week. Be here at nine tomorrow. I'll be in and out during the day, busy, busy!!"

He waved and went back down the stairs and Fen made her way towards the pub. She couldn't wait to tell Maisie and Jim all about her crazy afternoon.

As she reached the main road, she spotted Stella's shimmering hair and slowed down. She didn't want a conversation with Eggy, and had no desire to be brought back to the miserable mood of the morning, but it was his car that Stella was gliding into. Fen could see him in the driving seat.

But there was someone else there, holding the door open. The set of the shoulders, the way the soft brown hair curled against his neck, the sweet line of his jaw glimpsed as he turned. All the air left Fen's body and a small cold hand tightened around her heart.

Tommy.

CHAPTER FOUR

She had done so well for so long. Changed the subject if his name came up. Turned down invites to the cinema if he had a part in the film. Left the room if he came on television and turned the page if he was in the newspaper.

And now here she was, years later, pale as a wraith, pressed against the dirty alley wall and still feeling bereft.

She had hoped the denial would cure her, and somehow punish him. Making herself unable to be found, whilst knowing in her heart that he probably wasn't even looking.

The car drew away and Fen came out of the shadows. Her breathing was returning to normal and the pain in her throat had lessened.

'You stupid, stupid, romantic fool,' she chided herself. 'Just grow up.' The light of the day was fading now. She turned onto Dean Street and found it busy with people, off for a meal before the theatre, on their way home from work, meeting up with friends, their busy cheerful chatter jabbering around her.

She weaved her way through them, cold now and desperate for the solace of her bed.

Maisie was leaning up against the door of the Ann Boleyn smoking a pink cocktail cigarette. She spotted Fen and waved. Catching sight of her stricken face, Maisie took her arm and pulled her into the pub.

"God Fen, please don't tell me you were right about the sex thing. What has he made you agree to?" Her eyebrows knit in concern.

Fen gave a feeble laugh and tried to make her face look normal. She wanted to just tell Maisie that she had seen Tommy. But that would mean saying his name out loud, mean explaining, mean making it all real again.

The pub was already packed and it was difficult to move your arms. Maisie looked around for an ashtray, then gave up and stubbed out her cigarette in the lemon in her glass.

"Go on, spill the beans." She looked at Fen, screwing her blue eyes up quizzically. Maisie loved a bit of gossip and was always disappointed by Fen in that respect, unless of course she was drunk. Fen didn't want to be drunk now; she wanted to get away from the crowds and the shrieking of alcohol-induced gaiety. She could tell Maisie was well on her way to a long mad night, despite it only being Wednesday and work tomorrow.

"Geoff's given me a bit of work helping out the sound effects lady on that film. I just felt a bit funny out there, is all. Cold and no dinner."

Maisie's expression quickly changed to one of boredom; she had been hoping for scandal.

"That was sweet of him. Is it well paid?"

Fen realised she hadn't asked about the money. She hoped there would be some involved. The job had looked interesting, but not enough to do for free.

"I'm an idiot! I never asked."

"Oh, I'm sure he'll see you alright. Do you want a drink? Jim's at the bar. I can shout over..."

Fen shook her head. "No ta lovely. I'd better go home. New school tomorrow." She knew she couldn't cope with a night out with Maisie right now. They usually ended in a drunken carousal down the Embankment, looking for a late night drinking establishment which may, or may not, only exist in Maisie's sozzled head, then waking up on the floor in yesterday's clothes miles from home.

"Friday. Are you here then? We could make a night of it." Maisie put her head on one side. "Am I here Friday? You demented tart, I'm always here! I'll see you then, you party pooper." Maisie gave her a big wet kiss on the cheek and started to fight her way through the crowd to the bar, frantically waving and shouting: "JIIIM!!"

Fen had never before been as grateful for the bus stop being near her house as she was that evening. She almost cried out with relief as she let herself into the small grey brick terrace house and the sanctuary of her flat.

'Two bars for me!' She turned on the electric fire and warmed herself in front of it, turning her pale blotchy legs to red. The sash window rattled as Mr. Shah from upstairs closed the front door behind him on his way to his night shift at the sorting office.

Fen listened out for the comforting soft padding from above of Mrs. Shah in her slippers, but there was no noise.

Tonight must be one of the nights she spent helping out her son-in-law with his business, so Fen was all alone in the house. Warmer now, she supposed she should think about her tea. There was half a chicken and mushroom pie in the tiny fridge in the kitchenette; that would do. She unwrapped the pie and put it in the oven. While it was heating, she decided to sort out some shoes to take with her for work. If she propped the bedroom door open, she would be able to hear the telly whilst she had a rummage. Coronation Street was on and Ken was berating someone about something or another as she dragged all her shoes, indeed a great many, out from the bottom of the wardrobe.

She found a pair of school plimsolls, some old black high heels that she had worn once to an end of shoot party, some sensible courts that she'd had for her Christmas job and right at the back, in the corner were her 'We Live On The Farm' work boots that she had hurriedly stuffed into her bag on the day she had to leave the set.

The sight of them made her feel sad again, and tiredness and hunger welled up in her, along with the fat hot tears that spilled and plopped onto the cracked and muddy leather.

Fen sat back on her heels and pushed herself up.

'Enough of this you mad woman,' she berated herself.

Wiping her face, she pulled her blue and white holiday holdall down from the top of the wardrobe and stuffed the shoes into it, along with a couple of old shirts she never wore. Then she zipped it up and went to get her pie, stepping over the pile of other shoes left strewn across the floor. She would sort those out when she could be bothered, probably next year.

Fen took her pie and settled down on the chintzy pink sofa, feeling the springs sag ominously within. She had inherited it when her sister Sandy had opted to go all Ercol, preferring the cool modern blonde wood lines to the fat rambling roses and horsehair of the old Chesterfield.

She kicked off Wanda's golden ballet pumps and winced at the sight of her blood stained heels. She hoped there was enough hot water left in the immersion heater for a bath.

Part of a science fiction drama that Fen usually enjoyed, 'Out of The Unknown', was on and she longed to get caught up in the story and forget everything. But, although the actress playing the lead was even more beautiful than Stella and far more talented, the men were handsome and the music was groovy, Fen kept losing track of the plot and, when her pie was finished, she turned the television off, took a lukewarm bath and stepped over the heap of shoes in her bedroom doorway to go to bed.

Under the radioactive green glow of the hands of her alarm clock and the sulphur of the streetlight outside her window, Fen slept shallowly, woken briefly by Mrs. Shah's key in the front door and her quiet tread up the stairs.

Fitful dreams of giant knees and marauding bullocks disturbed her, and it was a relief when the jangling clock dragged her groggily awake. She hurriedly pulled on a pair of blue ski pants and a long black jumper; her hair was wild, but, as she was going to spend the day in a cellar, she couldn't be bothered to do anything about it and, even if she had wanted to, there was no time.

She jumped over the pile of shoes and ran out into another sunny spring day and then ran back in when she realised she had forgotten the holdall full of shoes. 'Well, at least I didn't forget my trousers,' she congratulated herself; not that she ever had forgotten to put her trousers on, but there was always a first time for everything.

The bus was packed with sleepy people on their way to work and Fen felt a pleasant kinship with them, at least until the novelty of standing squashed against a big man's armpit had dissipated. She felt nervous and excited as she fell out of the bus doors with everyone else in Oxford Street. The sounds of shutters going up and market stalls being made ready, and all the promise of a new start invigorated her.

Fen eventually found the door in the alley again and Simon let her in.

"Alright? Tea?"

'Monosyllabic always then', thought Fen. "I could make it..."

Simon looked at her as if she had just offered him a kidney. "Er, no, you go down. Wanda will be late. She always is. Thanks."

'Aha, the hint of a smile. I will break you yet, Mr. Sound Man.'

Fen entered the musty studio; her bloodied bargain shoes were where she had left them in front of the sofa. 'Bloody shoes,' she thought, sitting down next to them. She waited.

And waited. Simon popped in with her tea, and she wondered whether to quiz him about his life, where he lived and who with, but decided it was probably best to get the information piecemeal. Simon seemed as if he may scare easily and he had scuttled off sharpish to some technical room behind the studio.

Left on her own, Fen stomped about a bit on the wooden surface, then had a crunch around in the gravel, imagining herself walking up to a beautiful stately home wearing a flowing dress and a bonnet. She found a pair of coconut shells on the shelf and changed the daydream to galloping up in a tricorn hat.

Luckily, she had put the shells down and was fiddling with a beaded curtain hung in the corner when Wanda burst in, wafting away the must of the studio with a fug of sweet, expensive smelling perfume.

"Morning, darling. So sorry, my car turned up late."

'Car?' thought Fen. 'What happened to my car?'

She smiled at Wanda. "Good morning. You smell lovely." Best start with the sucking up straight away.

"Thank you. It's my signature blend, made for me by my parfumier."

Fen didn't believe her, but smiled anyway.

"I'll just get ready."

Wanda vanished for another half an hour and reappeared in her work clothes. Simon sat down to show them the last reel of the film.

Petie had managed to find out the whereabouts of the man with the iron leg from Stella (though Fen thought he might be quite obvious, having an iron leg and all), and it was a desperate race for her to warn him. The action took place mainly at a railway station, meant to be in Belgium, but looking suspiciously like Paddington. At the climax of the film, Iron Leg man escaped on a train as Petie strangled Stella behind a pillar.

There was a hush as the reel ended; no-one wanted to be the first to voice an opinion. Fen thought she had seen worse, but had also seen better.

"Well." Wanda broke the silence, having just remembered that there were no directors or producers present. "That was shit. Shall we do the moves first?" She heaped a pile of various materials on to Fen's lap; some silvery slinky lamé, an old flowery pillow case and a tweed jacket sleeve. "You do women. It's mostly that girl. Rustle about at the same time as them, lots of energy."

Simon came over and pointed the microphone at them where they sat on the sofa, turned the lights down and went back behind his console to press Record.

'This is very, very strange.' Fen vigorously moved her silver lamé as Stella's character ran across the platform, remembering to stop when the scene cut to Petie so that

Wanda could take over with half an old evening jacket. Then they were both rustling like mad as they reproduced the strangling scene. They had to stop a couple of times when Fen's stomach rumbled, much to her embarrassment, but luckily Wanda's did it too.

When they were done, Simon played some of the reel back to make sure he was happy with his levels. Listening to it, enthralled, Fen loved how the track made the characters seem as if they were talking to each other with their clothes.

"Feet now." Simon uncurled his cue sheets and went to rewind the picture.

"I suppose I'd better do all the main characters as you don't know what you're doing," Wanda sighed.

'Charming, but true,' thought Fen, but offered, "I'd love to try, if it would help and if you wouldn't mind guiding me, telling me where I'm going wrong."

Wanda was obviously wrestling between having complete control and the idea of having to do all the hard work.

"We'll give you a little try out," she condescended. "Pop those stilettos on and you can be what's-her-name walking up the platform."

There was a counter displaying minutes and seconds in red neon under the screen. Simon settled himself down, and asked Fen to move the microphone over to point at the stone floor. She clacked across in Wanda's shoes and waited nervously. Simon gave her the time that Stella's character would appear and told her to look for the blue cue line drawn on the print.

Fen geed herself up. 'So it's like dialogue. Start moving, not talking, on the cue. Don't mess this up.'

She clocked the time, saw the cue and put her foot down. Miraculously, the first two footsteps seemed to be in sync with Stella. Fen was so surprised and pleased, she lost concentration, missed the third foot, made a horrible scraping noise and stopped, feeling foolish.

Simon stopped the film. "Go again".

Wanda did look rather smug, but tried to be kind. "Don't over think it. Get into her rhythm," she advised.

On the third attempt, Fen could hear her feet clip clopping along at the same time as Stella on the screen. She even managed a nifty turn. She had never thought walking along at the same time as someone would give her such a sense of achievement. Wanda looked grudgingly impressed.

"Good," barked Simon. "Now henchman at 2 minutes 15."

Fen moved off the surface, wanting to do a little happy dance of joy, but deciding to save it until later. They tackled the background characters at the railway station next, which involved Simon telling them times and what colour cues to look for.

"Man in hat, right to left, yellow cue." In fact, there were so many cues on the print at times, it just looked like scribble, and most of the men had hats on. So they became a little more creative than Geoff Lewis had been in his descriptions on the cue sheets. There was beardy man, red hat, weird eye. Basket woman, no chin, left to right. Centre man, looks like duck, funny eyes.

In the end, even Simon joined in, and when lunch time arrived, everyone was in high spirits.

CHAPTER FIVE

They surfaced blinking into the sunlight. Except for Wanda, who was sporting an enormous pair of bronze sunglasses. She had also changed into an immaculately cut trouser suit and applied vivid red lipstick.

"Where's Geoff? Is he not buying us lunch?" Simon shrugged. "Don't look like it."

Wanda sighed. "Tiresome." She brushed an imaginary speck of dust from her lapel. "Leoni's?"

Simon mumbled something about having to meet his brother at Huntley Post and scuttled off. Fen wondered, as it turned out correctly, if his brother was the recording engineer she had seen (well, the back of his head) the day before. And also if they were part of some great sound man dynasty, or just grown in jars in a laboratory from a single cell.

Wanda had set off towards an Italian restaurant, its façade gaily painted green and red, ignoring the oncoming taxis and striding across the road towing Fen behind her. Struggling to keep up, Fen realised she had no choice but to follow.

Wanda burst dramatically through the doors. From the cries of 'Bella! Bella!' and the kisses, it would be safe to assume she had visited the restaurant before. Fen hung back in the doorway, aware that she had dirt on her jumper and that a few small birds could well be supposed to be nesting in her hair. Three suave suited gentlemen were leaving and she stood aside to let them pass, looking at the floor in the desperate hope of becoming invisible. Suddenly, strong arms wrapped around her and lifted her into the air. She let out an unbecoming girlish squeal and looked up into Petie's gorgeous face.

"Honey! Twice in one week! This must be a record. Are you stalking me? You know I can't love you back the way you want." He put on a serious face and she pretended to cry.

"We're making the sound of your feet and your clothes. It's my new job...." Petie looked a bit taken aback and Fen wondered if she had sounded too much like a mad woman. She quickly changed the subject. It was second nature to her now; she excelled at it.

"How long until you can be a Gladiator, then?"

Petie sighed. "Sadly, precious, it's been put back a month. Gives me a bit more time to get myself toga fit." He patted his incredible abdominal muscles and Fen felt a little faint.

"Still," he went on. "Those two lovely boys," and he pointed outside to the two suited men who kept glaring at Fen impatiently, "Have given me a little part." They both sniggered.

"Stop it. In an episode of some Science Fiction series they've been filming down at Chivergreen. I hope I'm an alien. I fancy being rubbed all over with green. Tom Godwin is in it. He can rub me all over with green any day."

Fen gave a strained laugh. Tommy again; the world was getting too small. She could see Wanda seated at a table by the window, impatiently flicking the menu back and forth. She nodded towards her and then to the waiting suit men.

"I think we're wanted."

Petie gave her a big kiss, and, with promises to keep in touch that they both knew they would not keep, she watched him sashay away.

Fen took a seat opposite Wanda and smiled brightly, thinking crossly 'you are indoors woman, take them off,' as Wanda peered at her over the top of her sunglasses.

"You never mentioned our gorgeous henchman was a friend of yours," Wanda scolded.

Fen unwrapped her cutlery from the napkin.

"Oh, not really. We've met a few times. He's like that with everyone." She knew not to usurp Wanda's status as the glamorous one, and to remember her place, so she played it down.

"You should have introduced me," Wanda sniffed.

'Now why on earth would I want to do that?' Fen mused, and noted the atmosphere becoming frosty again.

At least she wasn't being given any time to brood about the second instance of Tommy reappearing in her life that week. Wanda's ego must be stroked, and there was also the imminent worry of who was going to pay for the meal, always a minefield. Would it look obvious if she chose cheap things and a glass of water, and could she pay for her own? Or would she get the nasty things while Wanda ate lobster and drank champagne and expected her to split the bill? Or would she not go for what she really wanted and then Wanda would offer to pay? Maybe she should pretend she had claustrophobia, restaurantophobia, and nip off for a bacon sandwich from the café.

"Wanda, when did you start doing this job? You are so brilliant at it, you must get so much work. Do you have the footsteps market sewn up?" 'Hmm, all a bit gushy,' thought Fen, but none of it a lie.

Wanda leant back and started on a long tale starting with her girlhood in Cheltenham, several cruises, her two husbands, her great popularity as a dancer and all her admirers.

"A prince, how exciting!" was all Fen needed to say.

She had decided to hell with it, she decided she would order what she liked and chose the spaghetti ai gamberoni. She could always do a runner if needs be. Wanda had ordered a very nice bottle of white wine. Fen sipped at a glass parsimoniously, and Wanda proceeded to sink the rest. The alcohol was making her both maudlin and bitter. She had started bitching about her former work partner

"That Miranda Miller. I made that girl. Two left feet. Geoff was right. I CARRIED her!!" Fen looked around to see how much of an effect Wanda's shouting was having on the other diners, wondering if she was brave enough to shush her, but most other people were having a big old theatrical shout at each other too. Fen was getting the giggles about Wanda's generation and their alliterative names. Harry Harrison had a mention, Sheila Shilton, Larry Larson.

'Maybe that's where I went wrong, I should have been Fen Fomaine, ooh no, it sounds like nose clearing.' Fen's food was so lovely, she was more than happy to let Wanda go on so she could concentrate on stuffing her face. 'Must build up my knees, make them big and strong for footstepping. Well, if I get asked back...'

Wanda was talking about her special friend Luigi now, how much help he was around the house, helping her choose her outfits, taking control of the finances. 'Hmmm, dubious.' Fen realised it might be a good idea, for both their sakes, if she steered Wanda away from ordering another bottle of wine, and back to work.

"Yum, that was delicious. Would it be okay if we went back now? I'd really like to see how we get on with the strangling scene." She was making herself feel sick with this toadying, but needs must.

Wanda lurched upright. "Of course dear," and, on seeing Fen reach for her purse, insisted, "No, no!! Let me pay." Fen protested and was surprised how touched she felt. Wanda may be annoying, self important and touchy, but she had given Fen, a complete stranger, a chance and a way into her world when she was under no obligation to do so, and now she was paying for her lunch as well.

"My treat tomorrow then." Wanda swayed a little and waved a finger. "It will be GEOFF'S treat tomorrow, make no mistake!" They both laughed and Fen guided her across the road back to the studio.

Wanda didn't do much work that afternoon. She shouted instructions at Fen from the sofa and then fell asleep at around four o'clock. Simon and Fen managed to muddle through, finishing off the feet for the background people, in their various hats.

Simon was more mellow without Wanda's waking presence, and gave Fen advice about microphone positions and how to change her weight to sound more manly for the male characters. She still never found out where he lived or who with; she imagined him sitting cosily drinking a cup of cocoa with all his engineer brothers at night, and having a lovely chat about pre-amps and decibels and other such sound things.

Wanda suddenly sprang upright. "Man left to right!" she barked, just as Geoff walked in. Fen clutched her chest at the shock, impressed at Wanda's psychic and skin saving abilities.

"Afternoon." Geoff glanced at the footage counter. "I can see you're doing well. All on schedule for finishing tomorrow."

"It could go over, you know. There's some very tricky spot effects to do. It's a three week job really." Geoff just ignored Wanda; she tried this on every job. He didn't mind. He was freelance too and would try it himself if he thought he could get away with it. And he did sometimes manage to sell the unused magnetic tape spacing at the end of the shoot, to pay for his holidays in Spain.

"Yes, yes. You'll be doing it for free then. The budget's run out." He smiled at Fen. "And how's this one getting along?"

'Please say I'm good.' She felt the familiar fear of rejection that occurred at all auditions, which after all, she supposed, was what this day had been.

Wanda considered her words. The truth was that Miranda had already been spreading poison about her amongst the other footsteps artists. They were few in number and wanted to keep it that way. But working with Miranda, who was more of a Prima Donna and better established than herself, meant she could never be top dog. This way, Wanda could nap longer in the afternoons and have a little more control. There was always the worry that Fen could take all her contacts and oust her, but Wanda was feeling her age now and tired more easily. She had some money secreted away that Luigi didn't know about. Maybe she should let somebody younger have a chance.

"She has done very well."

Fen shot her a look of gratitude and wanted to hug her.

"Great, because I've just got the job as dubbing editor on a new ten part series, starts in two weeks time. We've been given four days per episode for footsteps, so that should keep you both busy for a while."

Fen beamed at Wanda. "Thank you so much, all of you."

"You're welcome. I'll be back tomorrow." Wanda had started to speak and Geoff talked over her. "To buy the lunch

Wanda, don't worry. Simon, have you got any loops for me?"
The two men left the studio.

"Don't let me down." Wanda looked stern.

Fen smiled. "I won't." And she knew, however irritating, however aggravating Wanda might be, that she never would.

CHAPTER SIX

Friday brought the rain, and Fen splashed her way to the studio, jumping away from the kerb as the taxis dashed through puddles. She was surprised to see Wanda's tall figure by the door. A balding young man with a sour expression was holding an oversized umbrella above her head.

"Where is that boy? Doesn't he realise it's tipping down out here?"

Wanda was jabbing furiously at the entry button with a scarlet tipped finger. Fen wondered if it might be a bit rude if she pointed out that Simon probably wasn't expecting her to be on time, as she never had been before, and decided to make a non committal 'ahumm' noise instead.

The young man started speaking angrily in Italian. Wanda fixed him with a steely glare and responded, "No, you can not take the umbrella, you have no hair to get wet. Now bugger off and pick me up at five."

Fen heard him cursing under his breath as he sprinted off through the rain. "Luigi?" she asked Wanda.

"Yes, he has financial business in town today."

"He seems nice..." Fen hadn't managed to sound particularly convincing. 'He seems like an oily little toad' were her real thoughts, but, thankfully, Wanda had spied Simon sauntering around the corner. He did a theatrical double take at the sight of her.

"Blimey, have the clocks gone back?"

'Brave man, Simon, brave man.' Fen stood aside whilst he unlocked the door, nearly getting an extra soaking from Wanda's violent umbrella shaking, and the three of them trooped damply down the stairs.

Fen realised she was on her own in still retaining any enthusiasm for the film. The other two had lived and breathed it for the last two weeks, and had already seen it at least four times. Wanda had given up on her plans of getting extra days work out of Geoff and was clearly just killing time before the free lunch he'd promised. But they plodded on.

The background lady in the station scene now had the sound of Fen squeezing an old straw hat added to her to emulate the large wicker basket she carried. Men with hats also gained newspapers and suitcases rattling by. Fen and Wanda blew whistles and wheeled trolleys about randomly to provide a background atmosphere and finished off the morning taking it in turns to clank the leg from the suit of armour for the man eponymous with the film's title. Wanda had to take over in the end, once Fen's sudden inability to tell her left from her right threatened to change the title to: 'The Man With Two Iron Legs Occasionally.'

One o'clock came and so did Geoff, bearing brown envelopes, a fat one for Wanda and a skinny one for Fen. Wanda immediately ripped hers open and counted the money inside, but Fen pushed hers into the pocket of her jeans to save for later, in case she was disappointed and her face gave her away.

There were even more cries of delight from the waiters in Chez Jacques as Wanda breezed in. Fen guessed that they probably thought she was a film star and not someone who had been grubbing around in dirt most of the morning. But it was nice to bask in her reflected popularity, and it meant they got a lovely table.

The producer of the film had joined them and everyone was being positive and saying how much they had enjoyed it, what a box office hit they could see it becoming. Fen glanced into his heavy lidded eyes; he didn't look as if he believed a word of it. Even Simon had joined them and, sitting next to him throughout the rather delicious meal, she managed to learn that he lived in Penge with his wife and baby daughter and was a keen golfer. Very keen, incredibly keen, the keenest. Mind numbingly, soul destroyingly, shockingly keen. But it did give Fen a chance to practise her nodding and smiling skills, and to eat her lunch without the distraction of talking. 'The best food is food I haven't had to cook or pay for,' she thought, pushing a garlic mushroom into her mouth and mumbling "oh" at Simon's tales of a birdie or an eagle or a pterodactyl or whatever.

The lunch went on for a long time and they were all quite raucous and unsteady as they headed back. Wanda suddenly stopped still in the middle of the road and declared, "Celery!!"

Grabbing Fen by the arm, she dragged her round to Berwick Street market. The stall holders seemed unbothered by the squeezing, shaking and listening to of various heads of celery and a couple of Savoy cabbages. Wanda finally made her selection and waved towards Fen.

"She'll pay." 'Cow,' thought Fen, glad she had some change. She didn't want to get out her pay packet in the street, in case a huge wad of money fell out. She laughed to herself at the unlikely possibility and trailed back behind Wanda, bearing the vegetables.

The afternoon was spent making noises for Stella's strangling scene by twisting and snapping the celery. They did it with such drunken gusto that there would be no chance of the audience thinking she might survive. They moved on to the final scene of the film, a fight between the hero and four thugs. Wanda beat the Savoy cabbages with sticks and Fen snapped the left over celery for the sound of broken noses. By the time they were done, the studio looked and smelt like dry coleslaw.

Wanda wiped her hands down the front of her top.

"I think we're done, don't you?" Fen felt a little sad, but she could see all the tension leak from Simon; he even started to whistle a little tune as he set about tidying up the salad mess.

"Can I help?" Fen looked around for another broom. Wanda had already gone to make herself glamorous in the toilets.

"Thanks, it's alright. We've got no work here for a bit. Few days to tidy up."

"What's in next?"

"A bit of dialogue." Simon looked grumpy again. "Then that Miranda's coming in on a job."

"Wanda's 'friend'?" Simon nodded. "Maybe she'll be better on her own. That one was better with you." He nodded at Wanda as she came back in. Fen smiled and touched his arm.

"Thank you Simon, for helping me out, putting up with a learner." He looked embarrassed. "No problem. Hope to work with you again," he grunted.

Wanda and Fen sorted out their shoes, waved goodbye to Simon and left.

Luigi was waiting impatiently at the door. He had left the car on a parking meter. "Goodbye dear." Fen got a kiss on both cheeks and a bit of a shoulder squeeze. "See you at Chivergreen." Wanda took Luigi's arm and they rushed off squabbling in Italian and English.

Fen opened her mouth to shout after her. She had remembered that she had no idea where Chivergreen Studios were. But as they were making such a noise arguing, she decided to save her breath. 'Maisie might know.'

Maisie was doing her face in the big mirror in the reception at Huntley Post. She looked prematurely summery, in a white broderie anglaise dress, a pink cardigan and faun sling backs. She saw Fen's reflection as she pushed open the big glass doors.

"What do you want? Tart," she mumbled, applying her lipstick.

"You." Fen tweaked her skirt. "You look delicious, like nougat."

"I'm sweeter and not so chewy. You've got vegetation in your hair."

Fen stood next to her and looked at herself in the mirror. There was indeed celery in her hair, and her nice red sloppy jumper that she had thought would double for work and an evening out had a dirty mark on the front.

'If only I was a proper lady like Wanda, I'd have been organised enough to bring something to change into,' she realised regretfully.

She started to pick the bits out of her hair and pretended to flick them at Maisie, stopping when Maisie gave her an evil death stare.

"You're not bringing that old bag with you, are you?" She pointed at Fen's holiday holdall full of smelly old shoes.

"Aren't you coming then?? Ha ha!"

Maisie gave her a withering look. "You can leave that under my desk if you want. No-one will steal it. It's rubbish. Have you been drinking at your creepy new job?"

"I may have had a few glasses of a mighty posh red at Chez Jacques... For free!!!"

"Ooh, get you. Who did you con those out of?" Maisie looked grudgingly impressed.

"Geoff. Actually, I think the production company paid in the end. It seems ages ago. Are you going to be much longer?

I mean, I know it takes a while..." Fen ducked as Maisie tried to dust her with a blusher brush.

Stowing her bag away next to a half empty bottle of gin, she imagined how disappointed a thief would be if they did steal it. 'Unless they had a shoe fetish.' She slumped onto the red leather sofa by the mirror and stuck her legs out in front of her, frowning at the mud on her boots.

People were leaving work and saying goodbye to the back of Maisie's head as she continued her preening. Fen had started to get a small headache and she was quite tired. The thought of going home and having a little sleep seemed very enticing. But she didn't want to let Maisie down. Not that Maisie would mind much; she had loads of friends, and if she couldn't find them, she made some new ones.

This was precisely why Fen liked her. She never judged, she never bore a grudge and she was always up for a laugh. There was the faint worry that beneath all the fun and the drinking lay a hidden sadness. Fen sometimes wanted to probe deeper, but Maisie would just deflect the attention back onto her. And she did have Jim; surely, Fen hoped, he must keep her safe.

Maisie snapped her compact shut and turned to Fen.

"Perhaps you might like to borrow some make up. Please, at least borrow a comb...."

Fen snorted. "You are a cheeky young madam. I have my own, somewhere." She rooted through her handbag and found a claggy looking mascara and a brush with most of the bristles missing. Looking over Maisie's shoulder, she made her eyes look a bit more lively and tried to tidy her hair, but the brush just got stuck.

They both laughed. "Shall I just leave it in, like a stunning new hair accessory?"

"It'll never catch on. At least you've dislodged the salad." Maisie dragged the brush out, taking a clump of Fen's hair with it.

"OW!!"

"Oh hush, you big baby. Right! Let the weekend commence!"

CHAPTER SEVEN

Shop lights reflected in the puddles; the evening air hung with the smell of beer, tobacco and Friday night perfumes. The hurrying people chattered with excitement and relief, hopeful for a wild night to wipe away the boredom of their week at work. Fen felt caught up in the bubbling excitement, pushing the memory of the inevitable morning after to the back of her mind.

She and Maisie wove single file along the packed pavement.

"Where are you taking me?" Fen shouted at the back of Maisie's head.

"Guess!"

"Ooh that's tricky. The Ann Boleyn by any chance?"

Maisie turned her head. "I have to be there. My people expect it!"

She barged past a group of young men hanging around the pub door, who looked admiringly at her bottom. Fen followed, wondering if they would do the same to her, but concluded sadly that they would probably just start talking about football again.

Maisie looked frantically around the packed pub.

"There must be someone here I can get to go to the bar for us. Damn, I should have brought Jim."

Fen squeezed herself into a tiny gap between some fat businessmen and a group of shrieking girls, raising her voice to make herself heard.

"Where is he tonight?"

Maisie stood on tiptoes, peering over her head.

"He's taken his Mum to the cinema, weirdo. Great!! There's Gary from the transfer bay. He loves me." She waved wildly, nearly spilling the drink of one of the shrieking girls.

"Oi!" A hard faced brunette stepped forward aggressively.

"I'm so sorry. Ooh, I love your necklace, where's it from?" Maisie skilfully attempted to diffuse the situation.

Fen chuckled to herself. 'Nice work.'

Maisie easily managed to placate the girl with flattery, and she resumed cackling with her friends. She also adeptly got Gary to buy them two glasses of wine.

Fen leant wearily against the wall. She was so hot she knew her face must be as red as her jumper.

'I can't move my arms in this squash. How will I ever hold a glass and a cigarette and my bag?'

She managed to take the wine from Gary and, by moving her head down and her hand sideways, had a quick sip. Maisie was flirting outrageously with him, all flashing teeth and fluttering eyelashes. Fen didn't know how she could be bothered. Gary was a pimply young man with the toothy look of a hare. Quite unaware he was being used as a drinks dispenser, desire in his eyes, he clearly believed it to be all his birthdays, a new bicycle, a big win on the horses and

Christmas. Fen felt a little sorry for him, glad that she had given up on love. 'How on earth is she going to get rid of him? Will she get rid of him, or will I just lean here all night, unable to drink or move?'

With little taps on his arm, a sultry glance and a great big flash of her engagement ring, Maisie successfully sent Gary squeezing his way back to the bar.

She grinned at Fen. "God, I'm good."

"You, madam, are a tart of the first water. Has feminism passed you by?"

"Bah, if it means buying my own drinks, they can keep it." She pointed at Fen's glass of wine, barely touched in her numb hand. "You're guilty by association, anyway."

Fen sniggered. "Well, I would be if I could reach it to drink!"

Maisie pulled gently at the sleeve of one of the group of men next to Fen.

"So sorry to bother you sir, but my friend here has a terrible skin condition and needs space for the air to get to it. You wouldn't mind moving a little would you?" He looked down at Fen with horror and she knew he had an urge to scratch himself.

"No, er, sorry." He moved aside and Maisie winked at her.

"Better?"

Fen took a swig. "Thanks to you, I am now a scabby pariah, but at least I can drink my wine."

The crowd started to thin out as people made their way to theatres, clubs and restaurants, or off to their suburban homes.

Maisie made a dash for a free table and Fen plonked herself down with a sigh. "I've never seen you move so fast. I'm too old for this"

Maisie settled herself opposite, flicking a beer mat at her. "Yes you are."

"Grrr, I'm only four years older than you," Fen scowled.

Pushing an empty pint glass, left by the previous inhabitants, away, Maisie mildly pointed out: "Yes, but I am the right side of 30 and affianced to my true love."

"Well, Jim anyway." Fen noticed one of the businessmen point across to the spare seats on their table. "Don't say they're going to come over here with their fat terylene bottoms!"

Maisie noticed at the same time. "Quick," she hissed, "Start scratching!"

Fen furiously rubbed her arms and the man that Maisie had moved away shook his head at his friend and gestured him to the other side of the pub.

"You may be very, very old, but you have to go and get me another drink." Maisie handed over her empty glass.

Fen snorted with indignation. "Am I a substitute man now?"

"You have trousers on, and I wouldn't know what to ask for."

Fen sighed and stood up. "I could teach you."

"My silly girlish head wouldn't comprehend." Fen picked up their glasses and tutted, shaking her head sorrowfully.

"I'm ashamed of you."

'I am invisible.' Fen considered the possibility that she might be going to spend the rest of her life leaning across the bar waving a five pound note. All around her, people were being served. She had tried her best theatrical loud voice, but still the barmaid never once glanced in her direction. Maisie seemed to have attracted some young men to their table and Fen noticed with dismay that one of them was sitting in her seat, the seat she had waited all evening for, the seat she now loved with a passion.

Maisie waved her back over. "Fen, you are bloody useless. Give the money to these boys. I'm sure they'll get served."

Fen wanted to protest and say she was quite capable, in this day and age, of buying her own drink in a pub, but her nice warm tipsy feeling had started to wear off during her wait at the bar. She had also started to feel paranoid, that she may at some unremembered point in her life, in a drunken haze, done something unforgivable to the barmaid to make her ignore her so.

The young man in her seat jumped up, smiling, and refusing to take the money she offered, went with his friends to the bar. Maisie grabbed Fen's hands across the table.

"Look what I got for you while you were away!" she hissed gleefully. "The blondie one's called Piers, he's posh and he says he's an assistant producer. The curly one's called Frank, and he's something big in frozen foods."

"What, like a side of beef?"

"I despair of you Fen Romaine, I really do. He can woo you with peas. You haven't been interested in anyone for years. What on earth did the last one do?"

'Nothing,' Fen thought gloomily, picking at the yellowed anaglypta on the pub wall. She forced herself to rally. "Frozen food Frank is quite pretty," she admitted.

"You're blind. He's gorgeous. Bit short, but you can't have everything."

Fen turned to look at the young men up at the bar, who, she was pleased to note, were proving to be almost as invisible as she had been. Frank, was indeed, rather lovely. Dark brown shoulder length curly hair, a firm jaw. 'God, it's as if I'm checking over livestock.'

"Handsome is as handsome does," she said tartly.

"Shut up. You have to like them. They can get us into a private party at Knight's Club," Maisie frowned at her.

Fen shook her head and laughed. "What I love about a night out with you is how I always end up feeling like a two bit whore."

"That's 'cause you are. Shush, they're coming back."

Piers's hair was very fair and his eyelashes were too, giving him a goatish look. 'He thinks he's delicious,' decided

Fen, realising from his quick up and down glance that she had been rejected as a possibility. Frank shook her hand with a warm dry grip and smiled into her eyes. 'But he's nice.'

The two young men had both been at the same public school in Surrey and had moved to London to share a flat in Knightsbridge. Fen could feel Maisie getting excited at the prospect of a night out with posh boys and guessed, correctly, that both Piers and Frank had rarely encountered women like them before.

"Well gals," barked Piers. Fen caught Maisie's eye and tried not to laugh. "Fancy a trip to this bash? Should be good. Quite a few stars coming."

They put on keen and impressed faces to amuse each other. 'Poor deluded thing.' Fen was finding it very hard, after half a bottle of wine, to keep herself from giggling. 'Maisie is rude to very famous people every day at work. And me! I'm Dora from 'We Live on the Farm', positively a worldwide superstar.'

The barmaid with the possibly unreasonable grudge against Fen clanged the ship's bell above the bar for last orders. Fen and Maisie smirked at each other, their eyes sparkling with alcohol fuelled mischief as Piers announced: "Time to party. Let's be off, ladies!"

CHAPTER EIGHT

They breezed past the queue outside the club and up to a bored looking woman with a clipboard. "Yah, Piers Mulholland and Francis Morgan, plus two."

Maisie and Fen gripped hands tightly, bursting with the effort not to laugh out loud. Piers was talking very, very loudly just to ensure that he was heard by all the beautiful people impatiently waiting. They were waved through into a plush corridor, the walls lined with gold flock wallpaper.

They waited a while at the cloakroom, while an impossibly pretty Japanese girl slowly handed out tickets for coats, with the air of one whose soul had recently died.

Fen peered into the smoky ground floor room of the club, where a rock band was playing. The lead singer seemed to be dressed up as a giant owl, and the music sounded experimental to the point of madness. The room was heaving with people though.

'Maybe I am too old,' thought Fen. 'It just sounds like a God awful row to me.'

A man in a black suit, as wide as he was tall, pulled back a red velvet curtain and ushered them up a flight of stairs.

The V.I.P. lounge was like a womb; soft silky jazz played and the thick carpet made no noise under foot. Plump scarlet chairs and couches with fur cushions skirted a small empty dance floor and two impossibly handsome barmen rattled their cocktail shakers behind a golden bar.

Maisie's eyes were wide with delight. "Shangri La," she breathed.

Fen found it difficult to adapt to the dim light coming from twisted metal sconces on the wall.

"I know these people, don't I?" She turned, confused.

"No, silly. They're all in that rubbish Man With The Iron Leg film that you've been making funny noises on."

Fen quickly checked round to make sure no one had overheard Maisie call it rubbish. She would hate for them to be thrown out before they'd even had a cocktail.

Or a canapé! A waiter had just wafted by carrying a silver tray laden with delicious looking vol-au-vents.

"Oh yeah! Of course. Look, there's old Iron Leg himself!" Fen nudged Maisie.

Gerald St. John, the grey haired, suave hero of the film, lounged drunkenly on the central couch, surrounded by lovely young women. Fen wasn't surprised that he seemed smaller in real life. Most actors did; in fact she supposed, should anyone ever have recognised her, they would have thought the same thing of her. There were only two people she knew in the profession who didn't, seem smaller, that is.

"With any luck, Petie might be here!"

She peered into the gloomy corners, but there was no sign of him.

"Boo, probably having a fitting for his leather gladiator skirt."

"What are you on about?" Maisie screwed up her face in confusion, then pointed unsubtly and shouted: "Look, there's that Stella!"

Stella was draped elegantly over the bar, her smooth face vacant as she gazed about her.

'I bet she's thinking about what she'd really like to be doing, uncool things,' Fen mused, studying her. 'Breaking wind loudly, or making a big mess eating a cream horn.'

Piers and Frank had managed to get seats near Gerald St. John.

"Here you are, ladies!"

Maisie grimaced at the fluorescent pink drink she had been handed.

"Don't be so ungrateful," muttered Fen. "There's an umbrella and a plastic monkey too."

She turned her attention to Frank, who was studying his girly drink with bemusement.

"So, you and Piers share a flat?" He looked at her, blinking slightly as he dragged himself back into his surroundings. He gave her a gentle smile .

"Yeah, it's his really. He likes having me around. I'm quite obedient."

"Well house trained?"

"I tidy up after him a lot. But he gets me out and about, meeting people. I'm quite lazy..."

"And you work in frozen foods?" Fen hoped he would ask her something soon; she had started to feel like a grand inquisitor.

"It's my dad's company. I walk about with a piece of paper looking busy mostly. Trying to make the staff like me, even though I'm the boss's son."

"I'm sure they do. And do you enjoy it, frozen stuff? Is it interesting?"

'Possibly the most inane question I have ever asked,' she thought.

He looked at her with his head on one side and laughed, a slow deep laugh that stirred something in her memory. 'I will not think of him now,' she chided herself. 'This is my new life.' She smiled back.

"Sorry. I don't imagine frozen food would excite many people."

"Depends what you do with it, I guess!" He raised an eyebrow suggestively and continued. "No, music is my passion. I play guitar."

"Oh really?"

Fen became slightly distracted at the sight of Maisie and Piers chatting animatedly. Piers kept trying to put his hand on Maisie's knee while simultaneously gazing behind her at the young models surrounding Gerald St. John. She drained the last of her sickly sweet pink cocktail.

"Shall we go and have a look at the band downstairs?" she suggested. "The singer's dressed as a giant owl."

Frank's brown eyes twinkled in reply. "Why not?"

The owl band had finished, and a man in a silver cat suit was playing a huge organ. Fen fought down the temptation to remark: 'that's a big one.' The room was dark and sticky with sweat; all around, bodies swayed in time to the music. Fen and Frank were pushed close together, panicking her slightly. He looked at her and took her hand, turning back to watch the singer. 'This is nice,' thought Fen, comforted by his closeness, enjoying his warmth and the touch of his hair against her cheek as he swayed to the music. But she felt detached, unmoved. Desperate to feel just a small tinge of desire, to feel normal again.

'That man has done for me.' Her eyes misted with tears and she clutched at Frank's hand a little tighter.

"Alright?" he mouthed. She nodded, miming to him that she was going back up to the V.I.P. lounge. He gave her the thumbs up, but didn't follow.

Fen felt only a faint surprise that Piers had stuck himself to the face of one of the young models, like a barnacle. Stella still sat in the same position at the bar, motionless as an alabaster statue.

'Where's that Maisie gone? She'd better not have abandoned me!' Fen looked around, worried. But there she was, smooching on the dance floor, wrapped around Gerald St. John. Fen heard a metal sound in her head every time one of his feet hit the parquet of the dance floor. Maisie spotted her, gave a little wave and an exaggerated wink.

75

'Poor Jim. Looks like she's finally bagged her film star.'

Frank swished through the curtain behind her and placed his arm around her. "Getting a bit crazy down there. What are the others up to?" Fen gestured to Piers and then Maisie.

"Bacchanalia." He gave her shoulder a little squeeze and laughed.

"I can see that! I need to head off, up early to see my folks in Gloucester tomorrow. Are you coming?"

Fen felt confused. Was he asking her home to meet his parents already, or to go back with him for the night? She suddenly felt exhausted and flat.

"Frank, no. I'd better stay and save Maisie from herself." She touched his cheek. "It has been lovely meeting you."

He took her face in his hands and kissed her gently on the mouth. "Poor sad Fen." He smiled and headed down the stairs, turning as he left. "You were good in that farm programme. I had a bit of a crush on you." The curtain closed behind him and he was gone.

Fen found a corner seat, and curled her feet up underneath her. The room had started to spin a little, so she closed her eyes. Wanda was clinking two glasses together whilst Simon intoned, "Rhubarb, rhubarb." Geoff was playing jazz ukulele. And then she was outside the big farmhouse, the sweet night scent of hay, a warm hand on the back of her neck and a soft breath on her ear. But the breath got harsher and the bullock plunged at her, shaking her like a doll. "WAKE UP, you drunken sot!"

Fen grunted and jumped awake. Maisie stood in front of her, hair dishevelled and lipstick smeary. She waved a crisp gilt edged business card in Fen's face. "La la la!! A film star loves me!!"

Fen rubbed her face and yawned, muttering "Hoorah" and wondering if she sounded convinced. Maisie grabbed her hand and pulled her upright.

"Come on, let's go before he comes back and gets too fresh."

Fen was bundled out of the club, clutching her coat. The cold early morning air made her skin fizz. She swayed slightly, standing in a puddle, watching Maisie dance excitedly around her.

"How are we getting back?" Maisie flicked at her with the card.

"Walking! Walking, lovely walking!"

'Oh joy.' Fen didn't know if she could still walk; her body felt heavy and inert and she quite fancied just having a little nap in the gutter. Plus, Maisie lived in Brixton and, the way she felt, that might as well be as far away as Mongolia, outer or inner.

"All the way?" She looked sadly at Maisie with pleading eyes and was rewarded by being hit about the face with the business card. Fen tried feebly to snatch it away from her. "If you do that again, I shall eat it, and you will never get with your film star."

"Ha ha!! I don't want him. I just wanted to know I could! He is old and his breath smells of mushrooms, and he wants me to go on a cruise!!!"

Maisie's dancing about made Fen feel dizzier. Perhaps walking about would be better than standing after all, though lying down would be best. Fen set off unsteadily and Maisie grabbed her arm and pulled her back.

"This way!!"

By the time they reached the Embankment, Fen felt a little more human. Maisie had been jigging about most of the way while Fen trudged behind her, squinting through one eye and wondering if it was possible that she could keep walking and fall asleep at the same time. Maisie still twirled around maniacally and was now singing loudly and badly.

"Oh, film star, film star. Will you marry me? With your Muskrat, wife and bum!! Oh no, sweet Maisie, I can not marry you, for I have no pants to put on!!"

"Put a sock in it. We'll get arrested for being drunk and disorderly."

"Duncan who?" Maisie stopped suddenly and looked over into the river. She peered closely at the business card for a moment, then proceeded to tear it into tiny pieces, scattering them into the river like confetti.

"What have you done that for?" Fen asked, shocked. "Does it say Mr. N. Oddy, Toy Town on it?"

Maisie flicked a final piece from the stone balustrade and smiled. "It's all fantasy, Fen. You should know that." She took her arm. "Come on, nearly at Vauxhall Bridge. Once we're south of the river, taxis won't have any excuse not to pick us up."

They both cheered when they eventually saw the faint orange glow of the For Hire sign appearing over the bridge. Falling into the back of the cab, Maisie told the bemused driver; "I could kiss you!"

Fen settled back onto the cracked leather with relief and groaned.

"My poor feet. They're my fortune now, you know."

"Thank goodness it's not your face or you'd be terribly poor. Brixton please!"

Maisie lived on the top floor of a house on a very steep hill. The floors were sloping and it felt precarious, as if the house was waiting to tumble into the one next door and push the whole lot down like a pack of cards. Fen lay prone on the brown sofa, dislodging a sparkly Indian fabric throw.

Maisie bustled in from the kitchen and thrust a chipped mug of milky tea at her. "Budge up." Fen sighed and grudgingly made room, warming her chilled hands around the cup. She looked at Maisie, sitting beside her, taking off her make up with cold cream and lobbing tissues in the direction of the unlit fire.

"So you won't be ringing Gerald St. John then?"

"Nah. Why would I? I've got Jim."

Maisie took out her earrings thoughtfully.

"I know I moan about him, but he's good to me, makes me feel like a beautiful princess. And I know you sometimes wonder if I drink too much and party too much because inside I'm crying and hiding from some miserable truth, but I love my life. I've strung out my youth as long as I can, but next year or the one after, I'll marry Jim and we'll live in a lovely house with our beautiful children. Then I can look back happily on my wild days and wilder nights. What would I really want from Gerry St. Thing? A few swanky parties, pandering to the big ego that compensates for the size of his privates. Then I'll be dumped for the next silly girl who thinks he loves her. No ta. Jim may be dull, but he's kind and honest and good." She paused and added, "So there."

She popped the lid back on to the jar of cold cream noisily and patted Fen's knee. "It's you I worry about. What was wrong with Frank? He liked you. Who is it that has made you so unhappy and closed up?"

Fen shrugged her shoulders, uncomfortable under the scrutiny. Who indeed?

She took a sip of tea, trying to buy a little time before replying. Maisie wasn't letting it go, though.

"What about that Stephen boy you used to mention, your friend from home?"

Fen pictured him on that far off summer day, fair hair and tanned arms, kind grey eyes squinting against the sunshine, waving madly as her train left the station. No promises made. 'Just as well,' thought Fen glumly. She would have broken them all for Tommy. "Steve? We lost touch."

"And there's been no one since then?" Maisie got up and pulled blankets and a pillow out of the sideboard, dumping them on Fen's lap.

"Don't tell me if you don't want to. I'll find out one day, even if I have to resort to torture! Jim's taking me to see Showboat at the Adelphi tomorrow night, or today night even." She pointed at the window, as a faint grey light of dawn crept though the thin curtains. "So. Please leave quietly! Don't forget to come and get your shoe bag from under my desk."

She kissed Fen on the cheek. "Night night, sweetie. Thank you."

Fen returned the hug and closed her puffy eyes. 'I really am too old to be sleeping in my clothes.' She tried to make herself comfortable under the blankets on the lumpy sofa. The muffled cooing of two pigeons on the roof, echoing down the chimney, made her head fuzzy, mixing with the beat of the blood through her veins that pulsed and throbbed in her ears. She had wanted to tell Maisie about Tommy, spew it all out like bile, be rid of it. But she had told once before, and it had ruined everything.

CHAPTER NINE

Huddled on the back seat on top of the bus, trying to smoke a cigarette without being sick, Fen felt awful.

'I'm sure one of those pigeons crept down the chimney and pooed in my mouth.'

She looked at the other people on the top deck, all clean and smiling, off to meet their friends in the West End and do some shopping. Swallowing down a bile filled belch reminded her of why she hardly had these wild nights any more. She reflected that nearly all of her peers would now be sending their children off to ballet classes or football training, their husbands out to get the weekly groceries, yet she sat stinking and hung over on the number two bus.

Her stomach rumbled, but the thought of food repulsed her. She threw her cigarette butt out of the window.

A lady, laden down with shopping, made as if to sit next to her, but took a closer look and moved on, muttering, "Should be ashamed of herself," under her breath. 'I am vile.' Fen wanted to apologise, claim it was a temporary aberration, really she was a pillar of society, a paragon of virtue, a woman off the telly. 'Perhaps better not.'

Two miserable hours later, she let herself into her flat, cursed as she tripped over the pile of shoes, and threw herself thankfully onto her lovely, inviting bed. The busy, bright day continued outside her window, the sound of traffic and passing footsteps bleeding in and out of her dreams whilst she lay oblivious and unmoving until the noises grew quieter and dusk fell.

Fen stumbled around her flat, trying to see through puffy eyes well enough to find the light switch, hoping and praying that she'd remembered to put money in the meter.

The light in the bathroom shone on her reflection, her face pasty and her hair flat on one side and coiled into a wild pyramid on the other.

'Just gorgeous.' She flashed herself a show business smile and admired the new wrinkles etched into her cheek from the bed sheets. 'Ugh.'

Wandering back to the bedroom, unsure if she would be able to get back to sleep, she noticed a folded piece of paper pushed under her front door. 'Ooh, hello, what's this?' She settled down on the sofa to read.

'Fiona! Where are you? Are you dead? Mrs. Shah let me in. She says she hasn't seen you for ages. Come to lunch on Sunday. Sandy might be coming, if she's not too busy. I'll pick you up at twelve, so no pathetic excuses about the buses not running. Love and kisses, Justin.'

Fen's mouth filled with saliva at the thought of her sister-in-law Patricia's delicious food, making her let out a little moan of greed. The vol-au-vents she had eaten at the night club seemed decades ago now. She decided she must try and get back to sleep.

She finally woke at eleven and rushed around in a panic, trying to make herself presentable. There was little that could be done with her hair; it was still freakishly lopsided.

'I'll go for the glamorous headscarf option,' she decided, wrapping a red and white spotted one round her head. 'Hmm, not so much glamour, more head injury,' she concluded, but decided it was a slight improvement on the mad, whippy look.

Justin was revving up his Hillman Imp and tooting his horn impatiently. Fen tried to open her front garden iron gate the wrong way for a few seconds and then got her bag caught in it on the way through and was snapped backwards. She could see her brother laughing at her in his rear view mirror. She slammed the car door shut, because she knew it annoyed him.

"Shut up, you."

His shoulders were shaking with laughter as the car pulled away.

"Graceful as ever I see, Fiona."

Fen knew she would have to quickly revert to being Fiona Rompton for the day. Her family refused to acknowledge that she was now Fenella Romaine, erstwhile drama queen and now star of the gravel pit.

'At least I get a lovely dinner,' Fen comforted herself, 'Even if I do have to be teased mercilessly all afternoon.'

Patricia stood in the doorway, fresh and bright, a flowery apron covering her blue checked dress, a tea towel draped jauntily over one shoulder.

"There you are! It's beef, hope that's okay. Sandy is running a bit late. She's just seen Doug off to Egypt at the airport." She patted Justin on the head as he passed her and made off down the hall. "Don't you go and skulk in that studio! We've got guests, remember!"

He muttered something about 'only family' as he disappeared into the garden. Patricia smiled at Fen, exasperated.

"Honestly, that man. And how come you and your sister got all the hair and he got so little?"

Fen tugged at her headscarf slightly.

"It can be a curse. How are you? Where are Tilly and Duncan?"

Patricia ushered her down the cool tiled hall and into the sunlit kitchen.

"Duncan is upstairs in his room building a space rocket out of Lego and Tilly is trying to dress Bob up as a fairy."

On cue, a Shetland sheepdog hurtled past them, his claws skittering on the hall floor, sparkly wings trailing behind him. He was hotly pursued by Tilly, her pale blonde hair flying. She stopped when she saw Fen and ran up to her shrieking, "Auntie Fiona!!"

Fen knelt down for a hug and a big wet kiss from her niece. Tilly examined her quizzically.

"Have you hurt your head?"

"No, I'm trying to be glamorous." Tilly paused. Getting close to Fen's ear, she hissed: "It isn't working" and ran off up the stairs shouting, "Fairy Bob! I'm coming to get you!"

"Can I do anything to help?" Fen asked.

"No, everything's under control. Just help yourself to a drink."

Patricia disappeared back into the kitchen and Fen poured herself a gin and tonic, in the faint hope it might make her feel better. She wished she could say, at least once, that her own cooking was ever under control, or indeed her life.

She looked through the French windows, down the long garden, still gleaming from early morning rain, to a large wooden building, the pale yellow paint distressed and peeling. She could glimpse Justin moving about inside, holding canvasses up to the light.

Her brother was held in very high regard by the art world. Unfortunately, his choice of subject and materials meant he rarely sold any paintings. He was, at present, obsessed with decay. His creations were large canvasses depicting decomposing birds and animals, executed with paints that he had made himself from rotting meat and vegetation.

'You wouldn't want one of those in your sitting room on a hot day,' Fen mused.

It was lucky that Patricia and her sister had inherited a thriving tyre factory from their grandfather, which paid for the beautiful three storey house in the leafy street in Highgate.

Bob started yapping at the sound of the doorbell.

"I'll get it!" Fen sprinted to the front door, the ice in her drink clinking against the glass. "Sis!"

Sandy stood looking distracted on the doorstep.

"Hello you." She bent her head to return Fen's kiss. Tall and slender, her wild hair tamed into a chic crop, wearing an elegantly cut dove grey trouser suit, Sandy did not look like the average academic, or a younger sister. At thirty years old, she was fast becoming the world's leading expert on Ancient Egyptian Jewellery with her work at Cambridge.

"Drink? How was the drive? Did Doug get off alright?" Fen led her into the sitting room.

Patricia popped her head round the door and waved at her with an oven glove. Sandy dusted some dog hair off an armchair and sat down.

"Yes, grapefruit juice, not bad and fine. How are you? We all thought you'd joined the Foreign Legion."

Fen handed over the juice. "Sorry. I got a new job."

"Great, what are you in? Theatre or television? It's not street theatre is it? Or please God not a mime troupe. I would have to kill you."

Fen laughed. "And I would deserve to die. No, it's behind the scenes, sound effects."

"What, big wobbly boards for thunder storms?"

"Kind of. You have to do it at the same time as the actors though, walking about, coconut shells for horses..." Fen trailed off, noticing her sister's bemused expression and realising it all sounded rather silly and foolish compared to university research. She rapidly changed the subject.

"How long is Doug away for?"

"He thinks two months, but there's a possibility it could drag on longer. I might go out and join him if I finish my paper in time."

Fen bit back the desire to ask, "The Daily Mirror or the Sun?" realising her facetious and pathetic attempt at humour would most likely be met with a withering stare.

Sandy smiled up at her. "Well done, you resisted the temptation."

They heard Patricia shouting down the garden for Justin, and then up the stairs for Duncan and Tilly and made their way into the dining room.

Duncan came blinking in, disgruntled at being dragged away from his Lego and greeted them shyly, taking his place at the table. Justin entered, with exactly the same expression on his face as his son, bearing a large joint of beef and a shiny knife.

He scrutinised the meat. "I wonder how this will rot down." Patricia, behind him with bowls of vegetables and roast potatoes, nudged him with her elbow.

"I'll rot you down if you're not careful. Go and get the gravy."

With all the extra helpings she scoffed down, it dawned on Fen that she had eaten three dinners to everyone else's one. Justin raised an eyebrow as she pushed her final plate away and rubbed her bloated stomach. "Hungry?"

"Wormy worms, itchy bum," contributed Tilly.

Patricia stood up and they handed their empty plates across to her.

"Stop it, Tilly. There's a strawberry meringue concoction, if any one has room." She looked pointedly across the table at Fen, who smiled back fatly.

"Yum. I think there is still a tiny empty place to squeeze more in."

The remains of the meal lay untidied across the dining room table and they lounged around, sleepily drinking brandy.

Fen needed someone to burst her distended stomach with a pointy stick.

"I'm dying," she groaned, "And on my death certificate, the cause will be listed as greed."

"Perhaps we should all go for a long walk? Help us digest," suggested Sandy. This was greeted with apathetic grunts. Tilly was busy giving her Sindy doll a bad haircut with some plastic scissors.

"Auntie Fiona," she piped up.

"What, niece Matilda?"

"When are you going to be on the television again?"

Fen slumped down further into her chair, not sure if she could ever walk again, let alone work.

"I'm making noises to go on the telly at the moment. So you will sort of hear me, but not see me."

Tilly frowned, and started trying to remove one of Sindy's fingers.

"Are you too big to fit into the television now?"

Justin laughed and looked his sister up and down.

"I think she might be sweetheart, after all that dinner."

Fen threw a napkin at him. "I had NO dinner yesterday, cheeky. I'm just stockpiling."

"Does oily Eggy know about this?"

Tilly and Duncan started tittering.

"Eggy smell, bottom blast!"

Patricia, trying not to smile, ushered them out of the room.

That's enough you two. Go and play in the garden."

"Eggy suggested I might like a change of direction." Fen thought that sounded suitably diplomatic, better than 'your friend's husband is a shitty git and I hate him.'

Justin looked concerned. "Do you want me to get Emma to have a word with him?"

Fen noticed Patricia stiffening a little, still not entirely comfortable at her husband's continued friendship with his old flame.

"No, no, it's good. A new challenge. I wasn't getting much work anyway..." Sandy put down her glass and stretched her back. "I wonder why they killed you off in that farm thing. I thought you were quite good."

Fen hoisted her bloated carcass out of the chair as quickly as she could. "Plot device I think. Must have a wee."

She could hear Duncan and Tilly shouting at each other in the garden through the open bathroom window. She leant her hot forehead against the cool glass of the mirror and breathed slowly. 'When will everything stop coming back,' she despaired. She sat on the edge of the roll top bath, looking glumly at the soft white towels hung neatly on the rail. 'And why did I eat so much food.'

Sandy called up the stairs to her. "Fiona, are you okay? I'm going now, if you need a lift."

Justin and Patricia waved from the doorstep as they drove away.

"I feel guilty leaving them with all that washing up." Fen moved a pile of papers from under her feet and tried to stuff them in the glove compartment.

"Oh, don't worry about those. Leave them where they are. I can take you back, if you feel that bad. I have to leave now, I've got a lecture to prepare for tomorrow, and if I take you home, Justin can get on with painting a pile of dead crows being eaten by a rabbit, or whatever his latest masterpiece is."

"I am a burden to you all. I could have borrowed Tilly's fairy cycle and ridden home."

"Oh shut up. Are you going to see mum and dad before you start this new job? You should."

Fen sighed. "Yes." The words 'Bad Daughter' hung unspoken in the car between them.

As they drove along the Sunday empty streets, they chatted about Sandy's work and the dig in Egypt that Doug was working on, and whether or not she could find the time to join him in Luxor. How being a female academic in Cambridge, competing against the male experts in her field, made it more difficult for her to be taken seriously. It seemed as if hardly any time had passed until they arrived at Fen's house.

As Fen was getting out, Sandy remembered something.

"I forgot to tell you. Mum met Mrs. Hammond the other day, when she was out shopping. Apparently, Lucy is in Hollywood doing very well. Are you two still in touch?"

Fen shook her head.

"Oh, that's a shame. You two were always as thick as thieves."

Fen pushed the car door shut and stood waving on the pavement until the car was out of sight. Trying to open the rusty gate the wrong way, she started to cry.

CHAPTER TEN

"Car parking is on the first left, madam." The peaked capped security guard bobbed back into the lodge house and the wooden barrier wobbled upwards. As she drove into Chivergreen Studios, she mused upon when it could have been that she might have changed from a miss to a madam. If it had happened at a particular time and day that had passed her by unnoticed, a sudden over night thickening of the waist and drooping of the eyelids.

She had recently returned from a few days stay at her parents' house, which had been both lovely and infuriating in equal parts as she had, by the end of it, regressed back to the age of ten. She had spent some time trying to explain what her new job entailed, and had been met with baffled eyes and furrowed brows. In the end, she had just muttered petulantly, "It's just coconuts for horses. Okay?" and they had nodded and gone, "Oh."

Fen parked her Sunbeam Rapier, badly, under a tree. Another lucky result of her dutiful stay away, had been the acquisition of her uncle's old car. The chrome was badly pitted, one of the doors was rusting away and there was a very strange squeaking noise, as if the entire engine was powered by mice, but Fen was hugely grateful to have it. She and Maisie had worked out the journey on public transport when Fen had gone back to pick up her bag of shoes, and it had involved a bus, a tube, a train and a taxi cab and leaving at the ungodly time of half past five in the morning.

Fen turned the car key and silenced the mouse engine. Looking at her watch, she smugly congratulated herself on being half an hour early.

'Wonder how long I can keep that up for?'

Hers was one of only six cars in the car park. There were names written in italics on white wooden boards, reserving some of the spaces.

'I bet Wanda's got her own spot. I could park in it and hide, and watch her head implode.'

Fen decided that would be mean, even though it would bring her evil joy. She slid out of the cracked blue leather seat and leant over to drag her bag of shoes from the back.

It was a bright morning with a soft, dry wind and the promise of later warmth. Fen looked around her, impressed, at the many white buildings surrounding a long, central, grand house with imposing wooden double doors. Three men dressed in white coats and gloves emerged, wafting with them the delicious smell of bacon. A milk float whirred past, bearing what appeared to be a model of half of the Statue of Liberty on its back. A man dressed as a court jester jingled by, chatting about income tax to a nun.

'Probably not a real nun. This is like fairy land!'

Fen locked up her car and tried to remember the instructions Geoff Lewis had given her over the phone.

'An organised woman would have written them down,' she chided herself, and then recalled that she had done this, but had used the piece of paper to stop a rattle in her sash window.

She came to the start of a long low corridor, with glass doors in the distance. Above the doors was written: 'Sound Department', so she guessed it was probably the right way and set off, her feet in their pixie boots making a lonely echo on the grey linoleum floor. She could smell floor mops and disinfectant. Old movie posters lined the walls and a huge teak clock above the doors ticked balefully, telling her she was still early.

The door was heavy, and Fen had to push her shoulder against it; with an angry graunch, it flung open and she staggered into a large, dimly lit, carpeted lobby. Around the edges were seven doors, each with a neon sign above them and a red and a green light beside. A cabinet, full of golden trophies, gleamed on one wall and stairs wound upwards darkly. Fen looked around for the studio she would be working in, finally spotting it in the far corner. The illuminated sign read: 'Theatre Seven', and the green light was glowing.

Inside, only the security exit lights were on. She could see a glass booth, filled with equipment. A soothing bubbling sound came from the fish tank; she caught glimpses of neon tetra fish glistening through dark weeds. The space seemed vast. She walked tentatively over gravel, then wood and suddenly, with a loud buzz, the studio lit up and a voice shouted, "STOP!!"

Fen turned, startled, and looked wildly behind her. Far at the back of the studio, a man was gesticulating at her from behind the glass of the control booth. He leant forward and pressed the talk back button.

"Hello, you must be Fen. I'm Gary. You can thank me later for saving you from a soaking."

Fen gave a little confused wave and looked down at her feet. She was one footstep away from a large hole in the floor. A green hose snaked in front of her and deep water bubbled sluggishly in the dark.

'If I had fallen in there,' she mused, 'On my first day, with new people, I would have been straight on a train to Ulan Bator and changing my name to Boris.'

She backed carefully away from the water tank, and held her hand out towards Gary as he strode across the studio to meet her. He grabbed her hand firmly in his and squished it rather painfully. His face was as red as his Hawaiian shirt and he smiled widely, displaying yellowing, tomb stone teeth.

"Lovely to meet you, darling. Geoff said there might be water in this episode, so I thought I'd fill her up."

He bent down, wheezing with the effort, and fiddled behind a curtain next to the vast projector screen on the back wall. With a little fizz, the bubbles stopped and he pulled the hose out and stored it away.

"Only had two people fall in it this year. Your mate Wanda was one." His little eyes twinkled at her. Fen laughed, grateful at his attempt to make her feel a little less foolish.

A tall, pimply boy had entered from a door far at the back, and was manoeuvring a long pole with a microphone on the end.

'I bet he's related to Simon,' Fen thought, and she was right. He introduced himself as Terry the boom swinger, and he was indeed Simon's cousin.

Larry, the man who was going to spend the next couple of months handing Fen things she didn't want to use, was right behind him. A jolly old man in his early sixties, he was Simon's uncle.

Feeling a bit left out for not having a name that ended with 'ry', Fen introduced herself to them all, and took a seat under the window of the control booth on one of the green tweedy chairs. Looking around whilst they busied themselves setting up for the day's session, she was impressed by the size of the room. 'Like church!' She gazed up at the high ceiling, clad with white tiles, yellowed by years of dust and nicotine. Long large protuberances hung down at intervals, looming like alien mind probes. Fen guessed they must be for the acoustics, and not just a crazy design feature.

Larry pulled back the long grey velvet curtains that ran across the right hand wall, revealing a line of doors of many different types all leading to nowhere, each covered with a multitude of knobs, knockers and bells.

Fen noticed a big iron gate; knowing that it would make an eerie squeak, she itched to try it.

Geoff Lewis arrived, still distracted, but looking a little more relaxed than he had in Soho.

"Fen! You got here alright? Are you impressed?"

Fen got up and caught one of the film cans that was slipping from his grasp. "Oops! It's great, a bit bigger than before," she laughed.

Larry grabbed all of the cans as he passed and took them off to the projection booth. Geoff glanced around the studio.

"Wanda not here yet?"

Fen didn't know whether to make up an excuse for her, say she was in the Ladies, or had fallen in the water tank and gone off to get dry. In the end she just shrugged and said, "Um".

"Suppose she'll get here soon enough." Geoff seemed resigned. "We'll run the first reel of the programme, see what we want you to do. It's quite good actually. They're still filming the interiors here, so I dare say we'll get kicked out if any of the dialogue needs replacing. Ho hum."

He winked at her and went to join Gary in the control booth. Fen settled herself back into the seat as the house lights went down and the screen lit up.

After a crazy opening title section, consisting of black and white swirling graphics, orange silhouettes of angular figures and a theme tune eerily played on a theremin, 'Beyond The Universe' began.

The story started with four characters: an elderly professor, his young male assistant, a middle aged government official and, Fen snorted quietly to herself, Stella, as a glamorous assistant.

They were in a stark, white tiled, subterranean laboratory in a post-apocalyptic Britain. There had been an inter-galactic war.

'Probably a bit too costly to film that bit. Best to just keep referring to it,' Fen decided.

Aliens, both friendly and hostile, were scattered about the bleak upper world, and it appeared that the story would involve locating the good ones and destroying the evil.

'Like most stories.' Fen moved further down in her chair, getting caught up in the excitement and trying not to laugh out loud at the first alien who appeared. He was blue, called Xintrog, and had a papier maché attachment on top of his head which wobbled precariously whenever he moved. Xintrog was holding someone hostage in an old windmill. The professor was bartering, offering a place on a space ship in exchange for the hooded man cowering in a corner. The alien capitulated. Grabbing the hostage, he pulled the sack from his head. Fen gasped as she briefly caught a glimpse of a familiar face, then the picture stopped suddenly, the film slowly burning out from the centre, just like the opening titles of Bonanza.

CHAPTER ELEVEN

Fen jumped as the door burst open and Wanda breezed in, exclaiming, "Morning darlings!" in a very loud, theatrical voice.

Through the glass of the control booth behind her, she could hear Gary's muffled tirade of rich swear words, some she had never heard before. The main lights glared on and Wanda looked about her, bemused. "Problems?" She raised an eyebrow at Fen.

"It all went a bit burnt…"

Geoff joined them, rubbing his hands over his hair, resisting the temptation to start ripping out what was left of it.

"Ladies, bit of a breakdown, have to get a new print from the lab, and Gary thinks that they can't get the projector working until after lunch."

Wanda picked up her handbag. "We will still get paid?"

Geoff sighed and nodded mutely in response.

"I think I'll pop back home again then. See you at two. 'Bye!!" and she breezed back out again, waving behind her.

Geoff smiled apologetically at Fen. "What will you do, dear? You could sit in my cutting room if you like?"

Fen pondered. "I think I might have a little look round the studios. If that's allowed?"

"Of course. Try not to stray onto any sets though. There's a nice garden behind the main house. You'll probably recognise it as the location from quite a few films."

"I'll have a look."

Fen wandered back down the long corridor, trying to understand her emotions. In the few seconds before the frame of film had been destroyed she had known those eyes. Dark blue iris ringed with black, the sweet curve of dark brown lashes. If he was in the series, he was filming here now.

Groups of men stood chatting in the sunshine, some tall and pale, dressed in white laboratory coats, others tanned chestnut brown, tool belts heavy at their waists. Milk carts were still whirring by, bearing their strange cargoes: oil drums, actors dressed as soldiers, half of a space ship nose cone.

Fen heard the double doors of the big house swing softly shut behind her. A ray of sunlight lay jagged on the marble floor. She could smell beeswax and beef stew. Above her, the large crystal chandelier sent rainbows onto gilt framed paintings: portraits of dogs, their mouths stuffed full of game birds; another of an Arabian stallion with impossibly sized legs. In front of her, she could see, through the finger smeared glass, a cool green lawn running down to a lake. In the middle, a majestic stone fish fountain spat water against the blue sky. An artificial stately home garden, all make believe.

She crunched down the gravel pathway, under an ancient monkey puzzle tree and through a low archway cut into a tall yew hedge.

Inside, a stone statue of Venus, yellow and white with lichen, stood drooping on a plinth, surrounded by lavender bushes and hedged with box. All enclosed, the sun was captured by the square of yews and warmed her back.

Fen lay herself down on a wooden bench in an alcove and shut her eyes. The cat wee ammonia smell of the box hedges mingled warmly with the sweet scent of lavender leaves. A single bee buzzed about, woken too early, searching for pollen. High above her, she could hear the lonely hum of an aeroplane, and the sound took her back to another day.

The buzzing of a small light aircraft miles above her in the blue sky, bees humming beside her in the hebe bush and the scratch of grass on her bare legs. Fen lay on the lawn in front of the farmhouse, her script abandoned beside her, and turned her face up to the sun.

The jangling rattle of bangles stirred her and a shadow took the warmth away. She squinted through a half open eye and sighed.

"Lucy, you're in my light. I'll never get my rustic tan at this rate. I'm only doing this to make your life easier."

With a rustle from her long purple dress, and a clank from her silver bracelets, Lucy, the assistant make up artist on 'We Live On The Farm' slid lazily down beside her, pulling back her long auburn curls and tying them up with a green scarf.

"Good, because three new cast are turning up today. The local post mistress, the farrier and best of all..." She left a small pause for drama.

'Really,' thought Fen, rolling over to face her, 'She should have been the actress instead of me.'

Lucy lowered her voice. "The vet's assistant."

Fen looked confused. "Is that exciting?" she queried.

Lucy gave a barely suppressed squeal of excitement.

"It's Tom Godwin, Britain's best new talent, just passing through on his way to Hollywood! Honestly Fen, don't you read any of the magazines?" Fen remembered listlessly flicking through a Sight and Sound last time she had been in the green room, and not taking any notice of anything other than photos of actresses' shoes.

"What's he been in?"

Lucy gave her a withering look, and Fen felt suitably withered.

"He's tipped to be the next big thing. After he's finished here, he's off to star with Megan Hanway. You've heard of her?"

Fen cast her mind around and remembered a film poster in Eggy's office of a stunningly beautiful brunette with the fragile features of a porcelain doll.

"Ooh yes, really stunning American girl."

Lucy twitched the hem of her dress grumpily.

"She's not bad I suppose. If you like that sort of thing."

'Almost all of the male population of the world and a fair few women seem to.' Fen decided to keep this observation to herself. Lucy was very lovely to look at, petite and feminine, with her beautiful mane of hair and tawny skin and eyes. No need to put any make up on herself, just saving her art for her clients. But she was rather used to always being the most desired woman in the room, something that often made her a little unpopular with the actresses she worked on. Luckily, she was very good at her job and, by making them look lovely too, generally won them round.

"Perhaps he will take me with him to Hollywood."

Fen smiled sleepily. "Yes Lucy, maybe he will."

Fen had a scene to film that afternoon. The set of 'I Live On The Farm' was all in one location, and the cast and crew were staying in a beautiful run down stately home nearby, just across the deer park. It had, until recently, been used as a school.

The offices, make up rooms and wardrobe were in the main farmhouse, with a make shift canteen in the cowshed across the yard. Up in a large field behind the copse on the hill, a wooden façade had been built for the exterior scenes. All of the interior scenes were filmed in sets in a huge barn. Every site was within easy reach of all the others, but they were miles from the nearest town, the nearest centre of habitation being just a small sleepy village with a pub and a duck pond. It was as if they were all marooned together, cut off from the real world and busy creating an imaginary one.

Lucy sat Fen down in front of the mirror in the make up and scrutinised her with a frown.

"Fen, Fen, what can be done with this hair?"

She pulled some bits of grass out of it and threw them tetchily onto the floor. Rummaging about in one of her many plastic trays, she found the right brush and skilfully began to transform Fen into Dora, the farmer's daughter.

Up in the fields, the scene they were shooting that afternoon was between Dora and her father, played by Bernard Harris.

The actor was a bit of a rogue, with an impish sense of humour, and had already made Fen corpse twice just by looking at her in a certain way. The director, Ted, thirty years in the business and largely unflappable, had started to look a bit fed up with the pair of them.

"Come on, you two. The light will go at this rate, plus it's egg and chips in the canteen tonight and I'm starving."

Fen stuck her tongue out at Bernard and shook herself through, gazing down the beautiful long yellow sweep of the cornfield, dotted scarlet with poppies. She managed to become Dora long enough to act out the scene, a conversation about whether or not part of the farm should be sold to a local, evil, land owner.

"And cut. Thank you every one, that's it for today. Enjoy the evening." The crew started to pack away the equipment as quickly as they could, looking forward to a summer evening of food and drink.

Fen and Bernard picked up their scripts and wandered companionably back down the field to the farmhouse. By the time they were pushing through the broken down gate he had her crying with laughter, telling her a scurrilous, probably untrue, story about a leading actress they both knew being found in flagrante delicto with a goat called Pepe. As she straightened herself up, desperately trying not to wet herself, she noticed, through tear filled eyes, a small excited group of women mobbing around a car.

Fen managed to compose herself and exchanged a look with Bernard.

"Looks like the new boy has landed, and the ladies are staking their claim." He pointed at Lucy.

She was at the centre of the throng, tossing her hair around and giggling loudly. Fen's heart sank a little. She was very fond of her old friend, but hoped she wasn't going to have to spend time picking up the pieces if Lucy got hurt again.

They settled down on an iron bench under a twisted apple tree. Fen really hoped the gaggle moved out of the way soon. She needed a wee, and wanted to get to wardrobe to change out of her wellingtons and dungarees.

'Shall I just barge through them?' she considered. But she wasn't in the mood for new people; with the ten main members of the cast and the twenty strong crew, a happy little community had been built up in the two weeks since they started rehearsals and filming, and she felt childishly resentful of these interlopers. The group surrounding the three newcomers started to thin out a little. In the centre was a kindly looking middle aged woman and a large balding man with a face like a cod. Fen pointed him out to Bernard.

"Is baldy fish man the one they're all swooning over?" chastising herself inwardly for being mean, but saying it anyway.

Bernard filled his pipe and delved around in the pockets of his tweed coat for matches.

"You are a bad woman, Fen. Serve you right if you fell in love with him now and had to give him a big kiss. In fact, I might have a word with the writers and get Dora to have an affair with Mr. Bartholomy the farrier."

Sucking deeply and blowing out a puff of plum flavoured tobacco, he pointed with his pipe at a dark head bent listening intently to Lucy.

"The object of all this desire is that young fellow me lad there. I don't know why they are bothering, poor deluded fools."

Fen glanced up, interested.

"Oooh! Why? Spill the beans"

"I never had you down as such a little gossip. It's definitely a romance with our farrier for you. Young Tom is engaged to Megan Hanway, not only stupendously beautiful and intelligent, but also the daughter of one of the biggest cheeses in Hollywood."

Fen couldn't help but imagine a giant Edam in a hat, then felt her heart sink a little at the prospect of telling Lucy that her golden boy already had a golden girl. Bernard stood up.

"The way is clear for us anti-social bastards to get by now. Look, they're being taken on the tour."

Fen watched as Lucy took the new boy's arm and dragged him towards the canteen cowshed, with the others following behind.

"Hoo bloody rah. My wellingtons are welded onto me and I want my tea."

Fen and Bernard ducked under the pink hanging roses around the farmhouse door and down the cool stone flagged corridor to Wardrobe.

CHAPTER TWELVE

Fen stood in front of the catering van, greedily accepting an extra dollop of baked beans on her plate, when Lucy crept up behind her and jogged her elbow. "Ow! I've spilt volcanic bean juice on my hand now, you moron."

Lucy grabbed a paper serviette and thrust it at her, taking her tray so she was able to mop herself up.

"Sorry, sorry! Have you seen him? He's divine!"

Fen took back her dinner and found a place at one of the long trestle tables. There was still a faint lingering smell of manure in the shed, which always made eating there a slightly dubious experience. She picked up her cutlery and stabbed her runny egg.

"I've seen the back of his head, but mostly you were stuck to him, obscuring the view."

Fen looked fondly at Lucy, who was leaning excitedly across the table towards her.

"Do you think you should maybe leave him be for a bit? Let him settle in?"

Lucy shook her head, long silver-beaded ear rings flying.

"God, no! And let some one else get their claws into him?"

Fen waited to finish a mouthful of ham before suggesting: "Isn't this a bit shameful though, lovely? Like you're marking your territory? You might as well do a widdle on him."

Lucy caught her eye and smirked.

"Saucy. I suppose I might be being a bit keen. But I think he likes me. He's been charming."

"He's a handsome actor. You've met enough of those in your job to know that you can't trust charm."

Lucy started to look a bit cross. She was never that happy to be told the truth. She took one of Fen's chips.

"I think I can tell the real thing, thanks very much. Don't eat all of those. Wardrobe can't let out your dungarees any further. I'm going to offer to walk Tom over to the house. I'm sure he'll be happy to accept."

She pushed back the wooden settle, scraping it on the stone floor loudly enough to cause a lull in the clattering cutlery sounds as people looked up from eating. Fen glumly watched her flouncing away.

'Oh, and how on earth am I going to stop her from making an idiot of herself again?'

She glumly dipped a chip in her egg, knowing the best she could hope to do would be to make Lucy feel better when she fell.

The evening air was still warm as the light faded, a clear sky with stars blinking through next to a round bright moon. Their legs swished through the long grass as they all spread across the deer park, sauntering slowly back to the house. Fen could see Lucy with Tom, nearly at the bottom gate, heading a small trail of giggling women from the offices. The sound of their laughter drifted back through the stillness.

Fen was walking with her screen family, chatting about the scenes to be recorded the next day.

In the programme, Dora had an older sister and two younger brothers. They walked along beside Fen, bickering and teasing in the same way as they did when in character. Bernard and his screen wife Hetty strolled arm in arm a little way behind them. Fifteen year old Sam, who played the youngest boy, was trying to understand why all the women appeared to have gone mad over someone who wasn't him.

"Fen, you're sort of like a woman. What is it? Can I buy it in a shop?"

She linked arms with him.

"If only. Half a pound of sex appeal please."

Tamsin, the actress playing her sister Bella, soothed: "It's because he's new. We've been cut off from the real world for two weeks and it seems like two years. He's bought the excitement of the outside."

"So has fish man farrier," Sam argued.

She considered this briefly and capitulated. "It must be because he's bloody gorgeous then."

Fen breathed the sweet night scented grass deeply. 'I am having the best time. I could do this forever,' she realised. Then she remembered, with a small pang of guilt, that she had only written Steve one letter since she had arrived and he had sent four.

'I shall do that tonight. Sit out under the stars, drink some beer.' Except, she realised, once she had drunk some beer, she would probably do some dancing and sing some songs instead.

Climbing under the iron fence, they crunched down the weedy gravel drive, past the empty dolphin fountain and up the grand cracked stone steps to the house. It felt like home to Fen, sitting in her room with the dark, ancient, worm riddled worn boards and huge sash windows. Once splendid, heavy curtains hung sagging from a pitted brass pole, a grand design of fat roses across them, peppered with moth holes. Two bulbs on the dusty chandelier left gloomy shadows in the corners. The foxed misty mirror made Fen's reflection the most beautiful she had ever been. She winked at herself and left to join the inevitable party.

As she mingled with everyone on the terrace, Fen had a sudden guilty realisation that there had not been one night, since she arrived, where she had gone to bed completely sober.

Candles in jam jars lit the balustrades and someone had started a small bonfire by the fountain. Three of the sound crew had guitars and one of the Sparks had made a small set of drums out of buckets and an empty oil can. It was quite a good job that Fen was often drunk, or the temptation to ram the drum kit somewhere painful might become unavoidable. Luckily, it was unpopular with a lot of people and met with loud groans every time he started. But because he was a nice man, and they were fair people, he was allowed to use it for three songs a night. This had all been democratically decided with a proper vote and a secret ballot one very messy night soon after they arrived, and had set a trend for the Friday parliament and election of King for a week. Fen was one hundred percent certain who would be crowned this week, and maybe every week until the series wrapped.

Lucy sat on the ground, leaning back against the balustrade and swaying slightly in time to the folk songs.

"Where's what's his knob? Has he managed to escape your evil clutches?"

Fen poured them both red wine into cracked mugs.

"Ted is talking to him about tomorrow's scenes up in his room." Lucy smiled dreamily. "I think I'm in love, Fen."

"Don't be daft. You've only just met him and you know nothing about him."

Fen wanted to be kind without being a killjoy. "And you do know he's engaged to Megan Hanway?"

Lucy's face turned steely. "I think that's just a rumour to promote the new film."

"But he will be off to Hollywood when he's done here. Perhaps you could just enjoy looking at him..."

Fen could sense that Lucy was cross; she had stiffened and was glaring over at the blazing flames.

"I'm a bit cold. I think I'll sit nearer the fire." Her tone was tetchy.

"But Lucy, I'm just trying..."

'Oh, strop off then, drama queen.' Fen watched sadly as her friend left her alone, storming away to join a group of the wardrobe girls by the fountain.

The voices got louder as they drank and danced. Fen could smell a suspicious cigarette wafting over from behind the rhododendrons. As the night drew on, Lucy came back to her, tipsy and abashed and grabbed her in a hug.

"Sorry Fen, I am a silly."

"Yes you are, a big silly."

Ted arrived at the top of the stairs with the three new cast members. He clapped loudly and the chat trailed away with hissing and giggles.

"Right people, I'd like to introduce the newest members to our little tribe. This is Melissa. She'll be playing the post mistress for a couple of episodes, and this is Lionel."

Cod man bobbed his head in greeting.

"He will be our farrier. Hope the horses don't kick you, Lionel."

Someone laughed rather over-hysterically at this and Ted pursed his lips. "Who's pissed?"

A murmur rippled amongst them as everybody went to raise their arms.

"Alright, alright. You're probably all Spartacus as well. Anyway, this, as I'm sure you know, is young Tom. He is with us as the vet's assistant until the end of the show."

Tom lifted a hand and nodded to all of them. Fen couldn't help but pull a face of disgust as Lucy waved coquettishly.

'Ugh, she should have a fan to simper behind.' She looked back to the newcomers, trying to discern their features in the candlelight. Tom had noticed her grimace. He smiled at her, a slow, sweet, lazy smile curving his beautiful mouth, looked straight into her eyes and turned away.

"Oh my." Fen couldn't believe she had said it out loud; she had not had the power to stop herself. Luckily, Lucy, thoroughly over excited, hadn't heard her. She grabbed Fen by the arm.

"Did you see how he looked at me?"

Her face glowed radiant with joy.

'Yes.' Fen tried to compose herself. 'He looked at Lucy, pretty Lucy. Not me. Oh God.'

"Did he darling? That's great. I can't really see much in the dark. I think I'll go to bed. This cheap plonk is giving me a headache. Have fun, don't get carried away..."

Lucy pleaded with her to stay, moaning it would be no fun without her, but Fen knew that wasn't true. And she was suddenly feeling so strange, as if all the breath had been sucked from her body, a sensation that somehow the world had irrevocably shifted.

Two of the lighting boys were playing a game of boules in the main hall, using makeshift balls made of gaffer tape. Fen hopped across in front of them, muttering, "Sorry, sorry" as they booed her.

She began the long trek to her room, up the stone staircase, along the dim wood panelled corridors, through a hidden door and creaked noisily up the secret stairs. She was so happy that, as a major cast member, she had her own room. This was the first time in what she laughingly called to herself her 'career', that this had ever happened. Usually, there were at least three of them crammed into a room in a horrible bed and breakfast. She thought she might have a good old shout when she got in; that would bring her back to her senses. And write that letter to Steve.

As she approached her room, Fen could hear someone furiously rattling a door knob.

"Bugger!"

She peered through the shadows.

"Bernard, are you too drunk to understand how doors work again? Oh."

Tom stood looking ruefully down at his keys. He glanced up at her from under his girl's eyelashes.

'Oh no you don't, Sonny Jim. I'm on charm alert now.' Fen gave him a wintry half smile.

"Hi. How did you get up here so quickly? Did you fly?"

'Did you fly? Did you fly? He will think you are an idiot, woman. But then, who cares what he thinks of you? He's just a pretty boy actor. You've met them before.'

She realised that she wasn't being as good at acting as maybe she should be, given her profession.

"No. No flying." Tom laughed and pointed behind him.

"There's a secret lift. Didn't you know? Well, more a sort of dumb waiter. Bit of a squash, but quicker than walking. I can't get my door open...."

He tilted his head to one side and Fen wanted to punch him for looking so adorably cute.

'Good, now he's annoying me. That's a turn up.'

"Let me have a go."

He didn't move far enough out of her way. She could smell his skin through the blue cotton shirt he was wearing, see the line of his muscles beneath it.

"You have to pull it towards you, turn and push."

The door opened and Fen stepped quickly out of his way, back into her own personal space. His room looked much cleaner and nicer than hers, she spotted resentfully, and someone had put fresh flowers in a jug.

"Thank you."

He raised one eyebrow and held out his hand. She took it as briefly as she could, frightened she might catch desire.

"Fen. Fen Romaine. I play Dora, the farmer's daughter."

"Tom Godwin, Tommy. I can't remember who I'm playing, but I'm sure he will be lovely. Thank you, Fen Romaine, for saving a damsel in distress. I'll see you in the morning. We can squish into the secret lift together!"

Back in her own room, Fen pushed her face into a pillow and shouted very loudly indeed.

CHAPTER THIRTEEN

Fen wanted to stay where she was. Cold grey light spilled through the gap in the curtains and she snuggled lower under the eiderdown, groaning.

She had two interior scenes that morning and her brain felt so fuzzy that she knew it would be hard for her to remember the words. Bernard would probably make her laugh again too. She sat up slowly and squinted through gummy eyes at her alarm clock.

'Five thirty. Ungodly.'

Through the draughty window came the smell of a summer morning, the promise of hazy heat to come. She staggered across to her bathroom, still pleased that her current star status afforded her one, and she didn't have to scurry down the corridor with her towel and her wash bag. She never wanted anyone to see how large her hair was in the morning.

Fen stuck her head under the cold tap and squashed down her short curls, teeth chattering at the shock. She pulled on a pale grey shift dress and her red sandals, cleaned her teeth, and set off for the walk up to the canteen for breakfast.

Lucy was waiting for her in the entrance hall, having rushed down from her room in the old servants' quarters. Fen knew that its location peeved her greatly. "Morning!" she trilled perkily.

"Eurgh," replied Fen.

Lucy was used to early starts; she never even had a lie in on her days off.

"I'm going to have my work cut out making you look younger this morning." She scrutinised Fen critically.

"What do you mean? I've even grown an adolescent spot overnight, just for reality. Are we the first up?"

"No, most of the crew have set off. Need their bacon."

"Yum, bacon. And a cup of coffee."

Fen was becoming concerned that, with the free catering and late night drinking, by the time the series was over she would appear on the credits as 'Outbuilding.'

"I'm going to be good today, eat fruit and leaves. Shall we run up?"

Lucy laughed at her indulgently.

"Of course you are, and you might turn your ankle in a rabbit hole if we run, so no. Come on, I've got faces to paint. Including a rather lovely one."

"Why thank you!"

"Not you. You know who."

'Yes.' Fen swallowed, recalling the strong dry palm in hers, the vividness of his eyes. 'I do. Danger boy.'

"Hello, you!"

Lucy was surprised to see Tom sitting by himself in the cowshed canteen, half way through a full English breakfast.

"How did you get here so early?"

Tom put down a forkful of sausage and looked quickly up at Fen, noticing that she was pulling a very grumpy face.

"I didn't fly."

"Did the special lift go down to an ancient underground train system?" Fen shocked herself at how hostile she sounded.

Unabashed, Tom answered brightly. "I found a bicycle."

Lucy looked very confused.

"Have you two met before?"

Fen shook her head. "No, no, only yesterday. Don't worry, you sit down. I'll get you some corn flakes and tea."

As she walked up to the truck, she could hear Lucy chattering away happily to Tom in the background.

'I must try and be nicer,' she chided herself. 'The poor deluded lad probably thinks that charm works on everyone.'

Despite her earlier vow, while her mind requested fruit, her mouth seemed to have asked for a bacon and egg roll. She ate it messily while Lucy dipped prettily into her bowl of cereal and chatted about nothing. Tom kept trying to catch her eye, but Fen wouldn't look at him, partly out of bloody-mindedness and partly because she suspected she might have egg on her chin.

Indeed, when Lucy sat her down in front of the mirror to do her make up, she had. Also, the spot on her forehead had grown to a gargantuan size and become redder and angrier than the devil himself.

"Oh, Lucy, please make me pretty for the cameras!"

Lucy whipped a nylon bib underneath Fen's chin and tied it too tightly behind her neck.

"I can make you rustic. You're not meant to be pretty. It doesn't say pretty on your chart, it says 'ruddy and wind swept', which is just as well with that hair." Lucy opened a pot and lumped a big dollop of brown base onto Fen's nose. "Rub that in yourself, I've got this bird's nest to contend with."

All rustic, ruddy and windswept, Fen mooched across the farm yard, her hands pushed deep into the pockets of her dirty dungarees, desperately trying to remember her words.

'Grr, there aren't even that many of them. Something about udder rot, myxomatosis. No, masturbitis, oops not that.'

"Mastitis!" she blurted out.

"Same to you." Tom strolled by her, doffing the flat cap wardrobe had given him to wear. Fen laughed politely.

'Bum,' she realised. 'If the sodding cow's ill, it'll need a vet. I hope Bernard's not in that scene as well. I won't stand a chance with those two taking the piss.'

Everything went very professionally and quickly, mostly due to it being a lovely day and Bernard wanting to go to the nearest golf course to, as he would always juicily mumble in his best sleazy voice, relishing the double entendre, 'play a round'.

Fen made her way back through the golden fields, sucking on a straw and wondering how best to spend the next three hours until she was needed on set again. She could hear a lark singing and the sun was warm on her face. She felt her heart lift with contentment, being paid to do a job she loved, with great people, in a beautiful place, and thought about singing a little song.

She was just deciding which little song might best reflect her mood when she heard the swish of feet running through the corn behind her.

Turning, she blinked twice and swallowed hard, trying to work out what expression to have on her face.

Tom charged down the field towards her, blue shirt, untucked and open, flapping behind him. He pulled up beside her, barely out of breath.

"Hello! Didn't you hear me back there? Ted asked me to find you."

Fen crossly dismissed the small pang of disappointment that he hadn't come of his own accord.

"What does he want me for?"

She set off walking and he matched her stride.

"Because the light's so good, and they forecast rain tomorrow, he wants to do our scene this afternoon instead."

"Oh right, thanks."

Fen sorted through her mind, trying to remember if she knew the words. As if totally in tune with her thoughts, Tom asked: "Will you help me with the script? I can't remember if I know the words."

He widened his eyes to meet hers and gave her a puppy dog look that made her want to hit him and kiss him in equal parts.

"We could go into the village. I bet there's a lovely pub with a roaring open fire." She couldn't stop herself from looking briefly at his bare chest and felt her mouth fill with saliva. She switched her gaze quickly to the sky, hoping he hadn't noticed her leering at him.

'God, woman, get a grip,' she chastised herself, feeling the blood rush to her face. She attempted a nonchalant laugh, but it came out as a strange, strangled, yelping noise.

"In this weather?" she squeaked.

Tom's eyes twinkled and he gave her an amused and wicked grin.

"A metaphorical roaring open fire. Oh go on, we could go on my bike, I'll give you a lift on the handlebars."

Fen felt herself deflate, knew she was losing the battle. What harm could it do? They were colleagues after all. He needed to learn his lines, and so did she. Surely it would be churlish to refuse?

"Go on then, but don't ride too fast over any potholes!"

In the garden behind the long low pub, they slumped over a picnic table, nursing two pints of beer and sweltering in the mid day heat. Inside had been dark and cool, a maze of small rooms with low ceilings, the walls peppered with old china plates and horse brasses. They had found two empty leather seats by the unmade fire, but became worried that these might be the designated places for some old worthies from the village and didn't want to cause any upset, or a fight, suddenly acutely conscious of their interloping 'filming folk' status.

Tom swatted wasps away from the congealed pickle, all that remained of their ploughman's lunches, with his script. They were both having trouble saying 'mastitis' without making each other laugh, which didn't bode well for the afternoon's filming.

Fen put her script down with a sigh and took a sip of her warm beer.

"How long before you go to Hollywood, Tom?"

He gave her a look of mock terror.

"When we finish here. I was over there before I came here, for fittings and a read through. Probably why I'm having trouble with this script. Too much going on in my tiny brain!"

Fen noticed that a couple of the local girls where staring transfixed at him. She felt a warm glow that she was the one sitting opposite, and basked in his reflected glory.

"You must be missing Megan."

He looked up and she tried to work out from the expression on his face what the exact state of their relationship might be. Angry with herself because she wanted to see a sign that it was purely platonic and professional, a smoke screen to hide the fact that the starlet really liked girls.

'Or he likes boys, hadn't thought of that, had you?'

Fen couldn't work out anything at all. Tom looked just the same, smiling brightly; his warmth could be love or he could be acting, she couldn't tell.

"I'll see her soon. We'll be sick of each other by the end of the shoot!"

"You've done so well for yourself."

'Ugh' thought Fen, 'I sound like Lucy.'

The local girls were giggling and edging closer. Their boyfriends, strong and rough farm boys, had started to look a bit fed up. Tom smiled and waved at the girls and stood up to leave, hissing to Fen.

"I think those lads might be thinking about setting fire to some torches and running me out of town with a pitchfork up my arse."

Fen giggled and happily took his proffered hand, allowing herself to be pulled upright. They swiftly scooped up their empty plates and glasses and left them on the bar. Tom retrieved his bicycle and checked it over thoughtfully.

"At least those bad boys haven't let our tyres down."

He pushed the bike up the narrow lane for a while and Fen walked beside him, the overgrown grass on the verge brushing sensually against her arms. Their shoulders touched on every other step and she had forgotten to recoil. She looked at him and tried to fight down a tenderness, a longing to push his heat damp hair out of his eyes.

'Motherly,' she attempted to convince herself. 'I feel motherly.'

She prodded him in the ribs.

"No, I meant it back there, you have done well. I mean how long are you out of drama school?"

He smiled wickedly. "I know your game, you just want to find out how old I am, you dirty woman. Four years. I'm twenty five."

'Ah, so very young.' The four years between them stretched like an age to Fen. She expected him to say something glib, about how he had been lucky, so it surprised her when he looked so thoughtful, suddenly older, and said: "It's been damned hard. I've been all things to all people to get this opportunity. I know people will say it's down to Megan, but that's not the man I am."

Almost as soon as the cloud had descended on him, it quickly evaporated away. He patted the handle bars.

"Now then madam, up you pop, don't want to be late back for filming, do we?"

CHAPTER FOURTEEN

Shrieking, they sped down the hill, hedgerows packed with cow parsley blurring as they streaked past. Fen leant back against him, his chin resting on her shoulder, feeling as fearless as a child.

When they reached the beginning of the long gravel drive to the house, the mood shifted subtly. Fen sensed a change, like a small sweet scent on the breeze. She clambered from the handle bars, suddenly guilty, feeling complicit in a deception.

'Lucy will kill me,' she thought. 'But I've just been for a drink with a colleague that's all, one who has a beautiful famous fiancée in Hollywood.' Yet still she felt vaguely adulterous.

Tom pushed the bicycle beside her, whistling tunelessly, their former ease with each other lost slightly.

As the house appeared around the corner, Fen wondered if it would make matters worse if she suggested they went in separately.

'He probably thinks nothing of this,' she chided herself. 'It's all in my poor tortured head.'

But he paused, as if reading her thoughts, turned to look into her face and raised an eyebrow, nodding towards the house.

"You go in first. We don't want gossip." He lowered his eyes and looked rather intently at her mouth, causing her heart to turn to mush.

Lucy was waiting at the top of the grand stairs.

"What have you done to your make up? You've got another scene in about half an hour. You do know that?" she wailed.

Fen rubbed at her cheek, conscious that she was blushing fiery red.

"And have you seen Tommy? I've been looking for him everywhere."

Fen wondered if it was possible for her face to get any hotter without bursting into flames.

Suddenly cross at the ridiculousness of her guilt, Fen snapped, "He's down the drive on his bloody bike. I'm going for a wash."

She swept past her friend, who watched her passing with her mouth open, taken aback, calling, "I only asked" in a confused and plaintive voice.

Fen slammed the door of her room behind her and lay down on the cool sheets. 'This stops now,' she told herself. 'I will not ruin this lovely time by falling for a pretty, engaged, boy.'

Yet, despite her anger at herself, she could sense a little bubbling of joy inside her. The warmth of feeling, acknowledging that it would come to nothing, was all in her mind, would end in her tears, but she no longer had the power or the inclination to stop it.

Clean and composed, Fen found Lucy waiting on the balustrade, sipping cloudy lemonade.

She rubbed her friend's hair.

"Sorry petal, I was hot and cross. Can I have a sip?"

Lucy passed over the glass.

"Grumpy mare. I found him anyway. He's walking up with us." Fen gave her back the drink.

"Good," she said, meaning it. "Tell you what, I'll set off now and you two can catch me up."

Lucy laughed. "Oh no! Do you mean I'll have to spend time on my own with him?"

"You enjoy. I'll see you both later."

Fen set off, musing that already she appeared to have claimed some sort of ownership of Tom in her mind, granting time alone with him to Lucy as a gift, a gift that was not hers to give.

Tom appeared on set, hair slicked back, wearing round black rimmed glasses. "Check my specs, Fen! Aren't they fab?"

She pouted. "I'm jealous. You get to take them off and put them on all the time and make the continuity girl's life a nightmare. And you can peer over them!" She was delighted that their earlier ease with each other had returned. Maybe it would be alright; she could enjoy her little crush in secret.

And her admiration for him increased as soon as the cameras rolled.

Fen knew the limits of her own talents. She had good comedy timing, mostly remembered her lines and took direction well. She had empathy and was generous to her fellow actors, never feeling a need to hog the limelight.

But Tom was in a different league. The character he was playing was shy, nerdy, fresh from Veterinary College and desperate to make a good impression. And that's who he became, and he took them all with him. Fen no longer wanted to laugh when he said 'mastitis', because he made it stop just being a funny thing. She became genuinely worried about the fictional herd.

"And cut!" Ted stood up. "Thank you ladies and gentlemen. Don't get too drunk tonight."

"Fat chance," muttered Bernard. "Tommy, my lad, that was rather good. I hope you're not going to put us all to shame?"

'He already has,' thought Fen.

Tom laughed. "I'm sure you can hold your own Bernard, or if not, get someone to hold it for you."

The older man chuckled and slapped Tom on the back. "Good lad. Do you play golf?"

Tommy mouthed 'Help!' over his shoulder to Fen as Bernard linked arms with him and forcibly led him away.

That evening, in the canteen, she could see Tom sitting in the far corner chatting to Tamsin, her on screen sister. His character, Harry, had been written as the love interest for Bella, the eldest farm girl. They were reading a script and laughing.

'Just like he did with me in the pub.' She wondered if Tamsin was feeling the same things that she had and then remembered with an icy stab of jealousy that, in their scenes, there would be kissing, not just talking about udder diseases. Acting kissing, but kissing never the less.

'And she'll get paid to do it.' Fen looked around for someone to sit with. Lucy must still be in make up; there was a scene still to be shot that evening. Tom cupped his hands around his mouth and bellowed "Flannella!" causing everyone in the place to look up at her.

Embarrassed, she sidled through the tables towards him, holding her tray high to avoid the heads of the other diners. He patted the seat beside him and she squeezed in obediently, smiling at Tamsin.

Tom threw a pea at her, which landed in her cup of tea.

"The lovely Tamsin and I have been discussing our hot love scenes."

Fen fished the pea out, scalding her fingers, and looked sympathetically at Tamsin.

"You poor thing," she joked.

Tamsin just smiled indulgently. "Well, lukewarm maybe. I'm off now you're here Fen. You can keep this idiot boy company. Got to write a letter to my loved ones, see you both later."

Fen suddenly worried that Tamsin thought she was being diplomatic by leaving them together, and had spotted a change in her behaviour towards him that Lucy might also see. Then she remembered, with a pang, that she still hadn't written to Steve. And that, really, what she needed to say to him should be said face to face and not in biro.

Tom sensed that something was troubling her.

"Do you miss your loved ones, Fen?" he asked kindly.

She pushed some mashed potato around her plate moodily and glanced at him sidelong. In the crush of the canteen, he was really very close; she could see the faint freckles across his cheeks.

"Maybe not as much as I should," she admitted.

"They are like little bubbles aren't they, these jobs? Hard to know that the real world exists."

He stroked a finger down her arm and she felt the blood rush to the place where his touch had been.

'This pretty boy speaks the truth,' she admitted to herself. 'Oh no! Maybe he's warning me off! He thinks I'm like Lucy!'

Right on cue, her friend appeared by the catering van, looking wildly about her. Fen heard Tom's small intake of breath before he muttered, "Do you think it's too late to hide?"

She laughed shortly, reassured, but feeling horrible at her disloyalty.

"Don't be so mean about my friend," she hissed back, instantly worried that she might have sounded too angry.

But Tom waved and called over to Lucy and then studied Fen's face pensively. "You're right Fen," he said, "She's a nice girl. You can be my conscience."

He stood up, leaning over the table to push a chair out.

"Lucy! How the devil are you this evening? Have a seat."

'Don't overdo it,' thought Fen grumpily. She wasn't sure if she wanted to be his conscience; there were other things she realised she would much rather be.

Lucy was flirting, touching her hair constantly as she chatted to them about her day, taking any opportunity to tap Tom's hand where it lay on the table between them. Fen realised she didn't feel very well; a tension headache was pulsing behind her right temple. She pushed away her untouched dinner, grabbing a tiny lull in Lucy's onslaught to declare: "I think I'll go back for a lie down; too much sun I expect."

As she rose to leave, Tom grabbed her hand under the table and she cursed herself as her fingers curled involuntarily around his. He looked up at her, blue eyes concerned.

"You will be down for a drink later? If you feel better?"

Reluctantly, she slid her hand from his grasp and smiled tightly. "I'll see."

Back in her room, lying on her bed and watching a cobweb wave slowly from side to side on the ceiling above her head, Fen tried to work out how best to behave. She liked to behave well, do the right thing, but she knew that this was going to be a struggle. The light was fading and the air through her open window blew cool on her face. She could hear the laughs and shouts of the cast and crew as they returned home, and found herself unwittingly listening for a particular voice.

'Steve, what to do about Steve.' She tried to focus her mind on practicalities. They had known each other for years; the subtle shift in their relationship away from just friends had been recent, and joyous. But now she knew she wished it could miraculously return to how it had been before.

'But how can it?' she realised. It would be spoilt now, and her friendship with Lucy too, if she carried on feeling like this about Tom, allowed him to keep flirting, getting under her skin. If Lucy found out, thought Fen, she would never ever forgive her.

'That's if he means anything by it.' Fen reminded herself forcibly about Megan, about Tom's career, what he would lose from a dalliance with her. She decided to get up and give herself a long hard look in the mirror. She stared crossly at her puffy face, pale beneath her tan.

'Why would he want you, you stupid fool, when he could have the world?'

Happier that she had put things more into perspective, Fen decided to brave the party beginning downstairs beneath her window. She selected a pink flowered tunic dress to wear, splashed her face with cold water and set off to face the throng.

CHAPTER FIFTEEN

Lucy kept glancing over as she danced in front of the bonfire, giggling with the other girls from make up and wardrobe. Three of the cameramen were playing Beatles songs on their badly tuned guitars again. Fen had begun to think that they didn't know anything by anyone else. She and Tom sat on the parched grass, their backs against the side of the fountain, their shoulders touching slightly.

"Where do you come from, Tommy?" She didn't look at him as she asked, just moved herself slightly nearer.

"Heaven, darling."

She sighed, unsurprised at the cheesy answer. He gave her a nudge, apologetic.

"Sorry. Not far from here actually, can't you tell?"

Now he had mentioned, it she realised she could trace the faint remains of an extra O in front of the I beneath his received English accent.

"Do your parents still live nearby?"

Tom began to pull thoughtfully at the foil on the bottle of Blue Nun that stood between them.

"My Dad died in the war."

Fen turned to look at his profile, saw a muscle twitch tensely in his jaw. She recalled how her own father would never talk of his experiences in the war, just wore them like an overcoat of sadness.

"I'm sorry." She touched his arm briefly. "I bet he was a hero."

Tom paused before replying. "I'm sure he would have been, given the chance. He was in Alexandria. He got bitten by a sand fly two days after he arrived. It got infected and he died of septicaemia. My mother couldn't really cope without him. She was only eighteen. Went off the rails. I'd see her sometimes in the town, drunk, shouting, hanging off the arm of various seedy men. She died of cirrhosis of the liver ten years ago."

He lifted the wine bottle and thoughtfully sloshed the contents around, scrutinising them as they glittered in the firelight.

"It should be a lesson to us all." He gave a short dry laugh.

"Who cared for you, Tommy?" Fen turned to face him properly, leaning her head against the stone.

"My Gran, as best she could. She was old, is old. And so tired. I was a bit of a git, different and angry."

Fen took the wine from him, their fingers brushing against each other briefly. She swigged down a mouthful and passed it back.

"Do you see her much?"

Tom's eyes misted over slightly. "She doesn't really know who I am any more. She lives in a home in Bristol. I have to keep working to pay for it, take everything I can. The film job should see it all paid for as long as she needs it."

They were quiet for a moment. Fen felt sad for him and selfishly sad for herself, with the dawning realisation of how unlikely it was that anything could happen between them when he had so much to lose, and then she became angry for worrying about herself. Discomfited, she wriggled, getting ready to bolt. Tom sensed the reason behind her movement and touched her cheek gently.

"You stay here. I'll tell you the sad and sorry tale of how I had to put myself through drama school, four jobs, one of them taking old, rich women to tea at the Ritz. Actually, that last one wasn't so bad. It beat cleaning the toilets at the Colonial Club and having retired generals coming on to me all the time, bless them! Some of them wouldn't take no for an answer. Apparently I have a splendid rear. And you Flan, how have you got here?"

"Just luck, Tommy. A happy childhood, two siblings successful in their jobs so I could lark about." She looked into his eyes. "Luck. Tell me about your ladies, you filthy gigolo."

So he did, with the accents as well, until she was howling with laughter at one particular lady, a Mrs Lampeter, who would constantly be trying to touch his bottom, so that he had to keep his back to her at all times, until she realised it would be just as satisfying, if not more so, to try and grab his privates.

Lucy and her friends came over, curious at the hilarity, and clustered around him. Fen leant back against the cold crumbly stone of the fountain and listened, laughing with the others, allowing herself contentment.

And so it went on, for another week. Hard days filming, parties at night. They would seek out each other's company. He would save a place for Fen at meals, Lucy mistakenly believing it was for her. They would sit in the same groups in the evening, ride laughing up to their rooms, squished close together inside the dumb waiter, chastely saying good night to each other on the landing.

Another day dawned bright, full of warmth and promise and Fen jumped out of bed, in a way quite alien to her, looking forward to the day. She knew the reason why; she had a scene with Tom that morning, an excellent excuse to spend even more time with him. Bright and clean, she skipped down the staircase singing 'The Sun Has Got His Hat On' to meet Tom in the hallway.

"Why are you so cheerful, you heartless witch?" He laughed at her. "We're going to put Beaky to sleep!"

"It's not real, Tommy. You do know that, don't you? Beaky is just an actor like you, though possibly a better one. He has his own room and wardrobe, and probably a fan club."

They strolled up the drive together, turning happy faces up to the sun.

"I think I might slip something into the syringe to make it real. Not keen on that Beaky, he always out acts me and he's more popular with the girls than I am," Tom muttered, and let out a devilish cackle, sending a passing woodpigeon clattering into the blue sky.

Beaky, a tatty looking border collie with a wall eye, lay panting in the heat, by the side of his handler Samantha. He thumped his tail on the ground half-heartedly as Tom and Fen approached. He played the part of Janey, the farm dog, managing his trans-gender role with aplomb.

Tom leant down to pat him, and Beaky growled quietly.

"See, I told you, hates me."

Fen and Samantha exchanged smiles.

"He is a wise and clever dog and a great judge of character. I'm off to wardrobe, see you on set." Fen gave him a fond wave and wandered away.

"Sleep well, old girl." Bernard's choked voice had set Fen off crying.

'Not much acting required from me in this scene,' she sniffed to herself.

She remembered when Patch, her family dog, had been hit by a car, carried wrapped in a checked wool blanket to the vet's by her dad, never to return again. They had told her he had gone on holiday, but she knew that they were lying.

Tom plunged the pretend syringe into Beaky's neck and, on Samantha's hand signal, the Collie played dead. Except that on Ted's shout of "Cut", he didn't open his eyes. Tom looked at the prone dog, then at the syringe and then at a wailing Fen, uttering: "What?"

All her recent heightened emotions suddenly got the better of Fen and she turned and blundered off the set, eyes blind with tears.

She ran, crying, behind the canteen and across a small flower filled meadow to the little copse, a place where not so secret trysts between the cast and crew members often occurred. Sitting on a mouldering log in the green clearing, she tried to pull herself together. A blackbird sang sweetly in the tree above her head and somewhere in the distance a harvester chugged melodically through the wheat fields.

'What is wrong with me?'

She wiped her eyes roughly with the back of her hand, smearing black mascara across her cheeks. This fact made her think of Lucy and she cried even harder, tears leaving tracks through her rustic foundation.

Then Tom was in front of her, pulling her up, wrapping her in a rough embrace.

"Fen, Fen. You didn't think I killed him did you? I know I can be all sorts of bastard, but I wouldn't do that," he murmured into her hair.

Fen shook her head, burying it into the hollow of his throat. She could smell cinnamon and the salt tang of his sweat; trying to speak, only a gulping sound emerged. He took her face in his hands and turned it up towards him.

"He isn't dead darling. He was a bit hot, is all, and fell asleep. God, that ruddy dog deserves an Oscar. It isn't just that though, is it? What is it, what's wrong?" He stroked the tears tenderly from her eyes.

"Poor Fen."

And then his soft mouth was on hers and she was lost, tasting the sweetness of his tongue. The sunlight dappled through the trees onto her eyelids, the heat of him drying her tears.

Eventually, they broke apart and gazed at each other silently. Later, Fen would rack her brain to recall who had been the first to move away.

Tom smiled and whispered, "Oh..."

She laughed shakily. "Oh indeed. That's us destined for Hell."

"It's warm there. We can toast chestnuts, get a nice crispy tan."

He took her hand, checking her face for tear stains, trying to rub her make up smooth with his thumb. "Come on blotchy, I'll take you home."

As they approached the cowshed canteen, Tom let go of her hand. Fen realised glumly that she had felt the loss of contact as a small physical pain in her heart.

She stood behind him in the queue for the catering truck, looking mournfully at the back of his head.

'He's going to be funny with me now. Start making excuses and avoiding me. He'll probably laugh about his conquest with the crew. Except he won't, because it's me, and they'll just go 'ugh'.'

Fen tried to shake her negative thoughts away, conscious that she was working herself into a tizzy and might make herself start crying again. Tom turned to ask her what she wanted, and, seeing her stricken face, quickly touched her hand.

"Stop it, you. Go and grab us a good seat, one with a lovely view, see if we can see the sea. I'll find you delicacies to eat, fine foods from the orient, things your sophisticated palate yearns for. Like pie. I couldn't help but notice that you're a girl who loves a pie."

He gave her a little nudge and she dutifully mooched off to find a spare table, daring to hope that it might not, after all, be ruined.

Tom was true to his word and brought over a very large slice of minced beef pie with peas.

"It was the last bit, so I thought we'd share."

They squabbled idly over who was eating the most, Fen unable to meet his gaze, conscious of how intimate the shared plate might appear when Lucy inevitably joined them. And join them she did.

Tom rose almost as soon as she was seated and declared himself off to the production office to make a telephone call to America. Fen felt her heart rise and sink at the same time, see-sawing sickeningly in her chest.

The office was, in reality, a broken down summerhouse next to the overgrown maze in the house gardens. The production staff girls were often to be seen running out shrieking, due to the spiders that lurked in the cracked and weathered wood. It was home to the only three phones on the whole set and written permission was required to use them. Fen wondered what could be so important that Tom had been allowed to use one.

'A call to Megan to say he loves me now!' the romantic Fen decided, and then her gloomy realistic side piped up with: 'Or to have a big old laugh about how many women fancy him, especially the one with the knees.'

Lucy was curious too. "Why do you think he's calling America? Ooh, perhaps he's breaking up with her!"

"Don't be so mean. That would be horrible for both of them." Fen tried to ignore the voice in her head screaming 'hypocrite!'.

"It's probably about the film, asking about a script and stuff."

Lucy looked chastened and crestfallen. "I expect you're right." She stared more closely at Fen.

"Have you been crying, Fen? Poor thing. What's wrong? Missing Steve?"

'Steve'. The name deepened her guilt. 'I am an awful, awful woman.' She shook her head. "No, no. It was a sad scene to film today and I got mascara in my eye. I might be allergic or something, my eyes won't stop watering. I'll be fine. Have you eaten?"

Lucy nodded. "They brought us in some sandwiches earlier. I've got some drops that might be soothing. I'll put them in for you. Are you ready to go home?" Fen loved how they all thought of the big house as their home now. She was not the only one whose real life seemed a galaxy away.

"Yes, ready to go home." She linked arms with Lucy and they made their way across the fields.

CHAPTER SIXTEEN

Fen came down late to the party. She had spent most of the evening sitting by her open window, letting the air cool her face, going over and over the events of the afternoon in her head. She veered from joy to misery as she relived the memory of the kiss. Joy that it had happened at all and misery at the problems it may bring, the disloyalty to Lucy, Steve, and to a lesser degree, merely because she had never met her and hoped, but doubted, she was an old cow, Megan. Fen knew that she was most miserable because she wanted it to happen again; she yearned to touch him at least once more.

She couldn't muster the energy to make much of an effort with her appearance, so she just washed her face and pulled on a tatty shirt and her old jeans.

She was glad of the dark of the garden, and went to sit by Tamsin and Bernard. Sam, her youngest on screen brother, was there, and they were trying to hide him from his chaperone.

"Bernard, have you got Sam drunk?" Fen tutted in mock disapproval.

"No, my lovely, Sam has got himself drunk. We're just trying to sober him up a bit. Speaking of sober, get this down your neck."

He handed her a glass of wine. She took it from him, not sure if she could be bothered to drink it. She could hear Tom laughing on the other side of the fountain, caught a glimpse of

Lucy's fiery curls and stared morosely at the ground. She was cheered slightly by Tamsin and Bernard's attempts to gauge the extent of Sam's intoxication. They were giving him words to say to see if he could convince his chaperone (who could be heard calling angrily for him from the terrace) that he was perfectly fine. His attempts at 'oesophagus' were endearingly pathetic and slurred. They decided it might be safer to smuggle him into his room the back way and went off with him protesting that he 'hadn't drinken a morsel' and that he was 'as sober as a jug.'

Fen wasn't alone for long. Tom stood swaying before her, broad shouldered, tall and utterly irresistible, his hair ruffled and his eyes glittering. She looked up at him and chided: "God, you're drunker than Sam."

"Why are you over here on your own? Why didn't you come and find me?"

Fen was surprised that he looked hurt and confused. She opened and shut her mouth and shook her head.

"What, Fen? Tell me."

"This afternoon. I.."

"I know." He pulled her up to her feet.

"Come with me, I'll show you some bats."

Fen followed him, wondering if this was some sort of euphemism she had never heard before, giddily excited.

He stopped by the maze and pointed up at a large old oak tree. Fen could just make out its twisted trunk in the moonlight.

"I saw them. Where are they? I wanted to show you bats."

She touched his arm, trying to quieten him. "They've probably roosted now. Did you see them earlier? Show me them tomorrow."

He stroked her face gently. "You are funny, beautiful and a world expert on bats."

"Stop it."

He stood back, bewildered at the distress in her voice.

"I can't."

Fen looked into his eyes, her own pleading. He smiled, slowly, and again she felt all her good intentions flapping away, roosting up in the aged oak tree next to the bats.

"I know Fen. I do know. We're here in our lovely bubble. This is our reality in this moment. And I choose you as mine in this world. I can't not."

And he was kissing her again, and she was lost, mumbling protestations incoherently until, in the end, she felt herself surrender. It would end in tears and they would be her own, she thought. But here, now, in the dark of the gardens, with the pulse of music and laughter beating beyond the maze, the scent of the parched summer grass, in Tom's arms, she didn't care.

Fen woke, shivering as the chilly dawn air blew in from the open window. She wriggled out from under Tom's sleep-heavy arm and found a nightie on the floor. Pulling it over her head, she noticed its musty smell and a moth hole, not to mention the washed out picture of Snoopy on the front.

'I am irresistible,' she thought, padding back to sit on the side of the bed. 'I bet Hollywood film starlets can't rival me in the seductive nightwear stakes'.

Tom frowned slightly as he slept, muttering something that Fen didn't catch, but hoped was her name. She kept watching him, his long lashes curved across his cheeks.

'He looks so delicious,' she mused.

Her heart filled with love for him, a heaviness in her chest. She wanted to sit in the dawn stillness and look at him for an eternity. But the sun was rising and she could hear the distant sounds of the house stirring.

"Tommy."

She touched his cheek tentatively. She dreaded what might happen when he awoke, feared he might look at her with shock, then make a dash for the door, blustering with excuses about having been very drunk. She had put his clothes tidily next to him, so that she wouldn't have to endure the expected shame and agony for too long, enabling him to make a quick get away. But he yawned loudly and flashed her a sweet smile.

"Morning, lovely Flan. Have you been kicking me in the head all night? It hurts." Fen handed him a glass of water from the bedside cabinet.

"Actually, yes, I have. Drink this. Your clothes are next to you."

She pointed to the neat pile and his expression changed. Face falling, he looked bewildered and hurt.

"Do I have to go so soon?"

She shook her head, protesting. "No, no. I don't want you to. But people are getting up. I thought you wouldn't want to be seen."

He put the glass down and rubbed his sleepy eyes.

"Damn, you're so sensible."

'Ha,' Fen thought. 'If I were sensible, you wouldn't be lying there, me lad.'

He pulled himself out of bed. The square of his shoulders made the breath catch in Fen's throat. Half dressed, carrying his shoes in his hands, he made for the door. Turning with his hand on the door knob, he grinned at her.

"Sexy nightie, by the way."

Fen clutched her hands across her chest, trying to cover Snoopy up.

"Come over here, girl. Give me a kiss."

Dutifully, she went to him, held him as if he were off to war. He ran his hands through her bird's nest hair, looking long into her eyes.

"Save a place for me at the table?"

He sounded unsure. Fen whispered, "Always," knowing that she would never be able to deny him anything, ever again.

He tried to open the door quietly, but it groaned loudly with a horror film creak, making them both splutter with hushed laughter. He tiptoed dramatically along the landing, pausing to wave and blow her a kiss at his own door.

Fen lay down on the bed, breathing in the scent of him that lingered on the pillows, wondering if it were possible to die of joy. The temptation to cross over to his room was overwhelming and the thought of the hours until she would see him again seemed interminable. Eventually, she managed to sleep, exhausted, grateful that she wasn't needed for filming until after lunch.

He was waiting for her in the canteen, Lucy beside him, an unwitting decoy. His face lit up when he spotted her and they exchanged secret looks throughout the meal and throughout all the days that followed. Joyous hot summer days. Fen laughed constantly and loved incessantly, hard and happy days filming, long drunken evenings and the stolen night times when she would wait for the secret knock on her door.

'I can not believe that no one has noticed something going on between us.' Fen lay on the brown grass, eyes screwed up against the glaring sun, watching as Tom played cricket. A match had been set up by Bernard of cast against crew. Unsurprisingly, the crew seemed to be winning; the cast seemed mostly concerned about not being hit in the face by the ball.

'Except Tommy of course.' Fen felt a glow of pride. 'Ninety nine not out.' As soon as the thought passed through her mind, a cry went up and Tom was taking his gloves off and walking towards the 'pavilion', a trestle table bearing jugs of pink lemonade and three types of cake. Fen had joined in with the baking and had managed to make a fourth kind of cake, unkindly dubbed an Edwardian Spong and thrown on the lawn for the birds, where it still lay untouched, leaden and burnt.

Lucy ran up to Tom as he approached, cricket bat under one arm, and launched herself onto him, throwing her arms around his neck. He steadied himself with his free hand on her waist. Tamsin lay next to Fen, fanning herself with an old copy of Films and Filming.

"Ooh, do you see that?"

She gestured with the magazine towards Tom and Lucy. Fen's heart fell as she saw the picture of Megan on the front cover, impossibly beautiful and fragile, wearing a nun's habit.

"What?" She managed to make her voice sound normal.

"Those two. I think we might have a romance going on. Haven't you noticed how they are nearly always together? I swear he saves a place for her in the canteen."

Fen dug her finger nails into the hot earth.

"Does he? But what about thingy?" She pointed at Megan's photograph. 'I am so pathetic. I can't even say her name. And look at her, all breathtakingly pure. I should be sitting here with horns and a big fat tail.' Fen felt a guilty flush rising from her chest to her throat. Tamsin turned the magazine over and studied it for a moment.

"Mmm, she looks cold though, beautiful, but not a lot of fun."

Fen wanted to kiss her, thankful that she had lain back down with the magazine over her face, unable to see the look of delight that Fen could not manage to mask.

"So do you think I'm right?" Tamsin's muffled voice asked again. Fen hunted around in her brain for things to say to put Tamsin off the scent or change the subject, wondering if a sudden loud cry of, 'What's that over there?' might do the trick, when, luckily, she saw Tom and Lucy heading towards them.

"Shh, they're coming over. Unless you want me to ask them."

She laughed, a little too hysterically, stopping abruptly, the laugh trailing off with a hiccup. Tamsin looked at her quizzically from under the side of the magazine.

"Swallowed a fly? You just watch them from now on. You'll see what I mean. Bernard's running a book on it."

CHAPTER SEVENTEEN

As the shoot drew nearer to the end, more and more people were leaving. Most of the extras had gone, replaced now by people from the local village. Some of the crew had left to start work on other projects or to go home to their families, all hoping that the series would be a success and that they could spend the next few summers in this idyll. The evening parties had become leaving do's. Tonight's was for the actor who played the local landowner, Ronald Wilkins. He was off to Stratford to play Polonius.

It had been a stifling day, dark clouds mustering above the horizon, grey against the yellow of the corn stubble. Fen had been filmed galloping about all afternoon. She was very fond of the horse she had been given to ride, a fat grey cob called Nutty. It was Nutty's last day too, and she had treated him with an extra apple before he was boxed and driven off down the drive, Fen standing waving forlornly until Tom had laughed at her.

The parties had been getting wilder by the day and tonight's promised to be bacchanalian. Ronald was Bernard's sparring partner, a bon viveur of great repute. He had amassed a secret stash of fine wines which he was preparing to unleash on them all. Tom was convinced he had found them in an old cellar in the house.

"I swear he has, Fen. He's been digging through the walls late at night, putting the earth in his socks."

"You're just jealous you didn't find it first," she teased, as they made their way down the stairs out into the garden.

She had put on her favourite coffee coloured maxi dress, the one she had been saving for the wrap party, but, somehow, tonight felt special.

'Who knows, maybe me and Tommy might mention the future.' Fen comforted herself that they should all be back next year.

'That's if he's not too famous.' A quiet echo niggling in her brain added: 'or married.' But she chose to ignore it, for now.

Lucy waited for them by the fountain.

"You look breathtaking," Fen complimented her, and Tom mouthed "Wow!"

Lucy's beautiful curls were piled above her head, held in place with a glittering jewelled pin, and her green sheath dress glimmered with faceted beads. She touched Tom's arm.

"Oh stop it. Look what I've got!" She reached behind her, the dress tightening over her curves.

"Ta da!!" She waved two dusty bottles of red wine.

"One for you." She handed it to Tom. "And one for me. Where shall we sit?"

"I'll share mine with Fen." Tom handed over the bottle and grimaced at her. Lucy flashed her eyes at him. Fen looked from one to the other.

'God, it's like a silent film. We might as well all start miming and be done with it.'

"Let's go by the fountain, Lucy." Fen took her friend's arm, feeling the animosity pulsing through her skin.

"Good plan! I'll just have a word with Ronald and Bernard. See you in a bit." Tom hurried off.

'Cheers, Tommy,' thought Fen bitterly.

Lucy perched delicately on the side of the fountain, trying not to dirty her dress. She gave Fen a pleading look.

"This sounds awful, and you know I love you, but could you make yourself scarce tonight?"

"Oh, yes, sorry. Er, why?" Fen handed Lucy the bottle she had opened for her.

"I think Tom's finally going to make his move."

Fen nearly choked on the slug of wine. Once she had stopped spluttering and Lucy had stopped patting her on the back with her ineffective small hands, she managed to wheeze: "What on earth makes you think that?"

Lucy smirked. "People have noticed. He's always with me every meal time, saves a place so we're alone together."

"In a room full of people, yes." 'And me, you fool. I'm always there, you soppy, addle brained twit,' Fen shrieked silently.

Lucy pursed her lips. "Well, he has to keep up appearances. I can feel it Fen. He really likes me and I know I'm in love with him."

Fen groaned and hit her head against the stone wall of the fountain, rather harder than she had intended, causing her teeth to rattle.

"I thought we'd been through this, Lucy. He's engaged to a Hollywood film star whose father is financing his next film. What would he want with us? I mean you?"

Lucy fidgeted angrily, plucking at one of the glimmering beads on her dress. "You talk to him a lot, Fen. You're like his sister."

Fen had a flashback to the previous night and wondered if Lucy could ever be more wrong about that one.

"He must talk to you about me," she went on. "Why are you being so mean? Are you jealous?" She gave a bitter laugh. "Oh that's it. You've always been a bit envious, haven't you? Is this what it's about? You want him for yourself?"

"No, I'm not jealous. You know me, Lucy. Even if I were, I wouldn't want to ruin your chances. I'm just concerned."

Fen could see Tom in the distance, laughing his head off, without a care in the world.

'Come and help me, you sod.' She sent out a silent plea, but it seemed Tom was far too drunk to pick up the sonar. She looked at Lucy's sad flower face, deflated from her previous elation at the promise she had imagined the evening to hold. Fen took her hand.

"I don't know what I can do," she sighed.

Lucy perked up a little. "You could have a word with him. Everyone is saying he's interested: Bernard, Tamsin, Ronald. Perhaps he's shy."

Fen snorted with laughter. "Him? Shy? He's a lot of things, but shy isn't one of them."

Her head was beginning to hurt, partly from the over zealous knock on the wall and partly because of the muggy closeness of the night air. The red wine she was guzzling down was playing its part too. Lucy seemed close to tears now and Fen felt awful.

"Go and get him Fen. Tell him to come over and I'll tell him how I feel. I know he feels the same. Please do it for me. Why won't you?"

"Because I don't want you to be hurt."

'Like I will be.' Fen could feel her temples pounding. If this went on, she might go screaming mad and push Lucy in the fountain.

"That's not up to you, and I know I won't be. Oh, I'll get him myself." Lucy stood up and was pulled back sharply by Fen's grip on her elbow.

"Ow! Fen, what's wrong with you?"

"Tom is." 'Oh no I said that out loud.' She stood shakily. Lucy looked at her, green eyes confused.

"I don't understand. Tom is what?"

"Sleeping with me."

The rain started then. 'By rights there should be a flash of lightning,' Fen thought dramatically. And her wish was granted as thunder growled overhead and people started running for the house. Tom was still dancing around, singing. Lucy was glaring at her, incredulous.

"You're joking." Her voice was very small, barely audible above the torrential splattering of raindrops into the fountain.

"I'm so sorry."

They stood, their sodden party dresses hanging limply, careful party hair dressing lank on their faces. Lucy made a sudden dart to leave and Fen chased after her, shouting into the storm.

"Please don't say anything to the others. I didn't mean it to happen. I wouldn't hurt you for the world."

Lucy turned on her, fists clenched with rage.

"But you have. You have deceived me. You were my oldest friend and you let me make a fool of myself. Were the two of you laughing at me?"

Fen decided it might not be politic to admit that Tom had been, a bit.

"I would never do that. You must know."

Lucy looked her up and down and spat scathingly. "Seems I don't know anything about you. Bitch."

She stormed up the steps into the main hall, Fen following close behind. The harsh glare of the strip light made them both blink, mascara mixed with rain and tears running down both of their faces. Fen reached out.

"I am so, so sorry."

Lucy looked straight past her, her features contorted. Tom was rolling through the main doors, dripping wet, very drunk, wearing a battered straw hat and singing 'Knees up Mother Brown' in a rich and operatic baritone.

"Ladies! Have you missed me?" he cried cheerily.

Lucy looked at him with pure venom masking her hurt.

"Bastard!" Her parting shot as she ran wailing up the stairs.

Tom's eyes darted from her to Fen, taking in Fen's tear stained worried face. He looked wildly about them. She could sense his relief on realising that everyone else had already gone into the sitting room and was making far too much racket to have heard anything.

"What have you done, Fen?" He looked so angry, she started to cry hard.

"I had to tell her. She thought you and her... She begged me to help her. I..." She hiccupped through her tears, desperate for him to hold her, say it was alright, that it didn't matter. But he was icy cold with rage.

"You stupid, stupid fool. What if she tells someone? I could lose everything." Fen had started to shake, her limbs trembling uncontrollably.

"She won't, I'll talk to her. I'll make it better. I'm sorry."

He hit his palm hard onto his forehead, angry with himself now.

"Oh go to bed, Fen, and keep your mouth shut, if you can. Quickly, before anyone comes out."

Fen turned and charged up the grand stone staircase, sobbing as quietly as she could manage, her heart in pieces.

CHAPTER EIGHTEEN

She waited to hear the quiet knock on the door, above the raging of the thunderstorm, but it never came. Eyes puffy and wide open, hugging herself tightly, she listened as the thunder retreated over the hills, until the cold fresh dawn filtered through the open window. Heavily, she dressed herself for the day's filming, wishing she could pretend to be ill and hide her misery from the world. Preparing herself to act all day, on and off set, she emerged into the savage hot sun, blazing up from the gravel drive.

'Thank God for sunglasses, and,' she added to herself, 'Thank God Tommy's not filming today.'

She felt another tear squeeze from her right eye. She couldn't understand how there was any liquid left in her body. She felt arid and finished.

Down the cool passage way to make up, her heart started to race.

'Please let her forgive me,' Fen thought. Another guilty wave started as she knew what she really hoped for was that Lucy wouldn't have told anyone, that everything would be the same as before, that Tom would still want her.

Fen removed her big black sunglasses cautiously and looked about her at the empty seats and mirrors. The door to the back of the room opened and she braced herself. But it was Natalie, one of the trainees.

"Hi there, Fen!" she trilled cheerfully. "Have a seat. That storm was crazy yesterday, wasn't it?"

She did a double take on seeing Fen's pale swollen face.

"Blimey, you must have put away a lot last night! Still, at least you've turned up. Lucy says she's sick. Lightweight!"

She swished a nylon cape around Fen's neck and started to search through the tray of foundations. Fen tried not to look at her own reflection in the mirror, hoping that Natalie could find a pan stick called 'misery begone' or 'I have not been having an affair with my engaged co-star, whom my best friend believes herself to be in love with, and who now hates me.'

Natalie turned back with a flourish. "I think this might cover your multitude of sins!"

Fen bared her teeth in what she optimistically believed resembled a perfectly natural smile. "It will take more than that Natalie, believe me."

Natalie laughed and started to rub the make up vigorously over Fen's face.

Fen relaxed slightly, happy to be able to close her eyes for a moment.

'She doesn't know. Lucy hasn't told her. Maybe Lucy will be a better person than me.'

During the morning's filming, everyone seemed to be behaving as normal. Her scenes were in the farmhouse with Bernard and her on-screen brothers, all a little tired from a disturbed night's sleep. The boys were teasing their elders on their fragile state, until Bernard reminded Sam of his recent experience with alcohol and he went a little pink and shut up.

Fen tried really hard not to look for Tom in the canteen, but her eyes darted surreptitiously about the cowshed despite herself. He wasn't there.

She sat with the others; the risotto she tried to eat tasted like dust. She laughed in all the right places, even managed a nonchalant "I don't know" when asked what Tom was up to that day, and what was wrong with Lucy. Smiled brightly at the innuendos and suggestions that they might be together getting up to no good, and thankfully went back to work for the afternoon.

At six o'clock, Fen managed her line: "I must just check on the bullocks" without the boys tittering, and they were all finished. They all went back to make up and started to wipe their faces clean. Bernard chucked a lump of dirty cotton wool over Fen's head in the direction of the bin. It missed and Natalie tutted at him as she bent to retrieve it.

"You did that on purpose, you old letch," she accused him.

"What can I say, Natalie, you bending over delights my aged heart."

Fen shook her head. "Bernard, you are a dirty old ram," she admonished.

He smiled, unabashed. "Guilty as charged. You finished now, lovely? Coming for dinner?"

Fen stood and leant closer to the mirror. 'I look almost normal now, who would ever know that I'm broken?' She tried to find comfort in the fact that her outside mask was standing up to the strain.

"No, I feel a bit washed out from last night. Maybe I've got the same thing as Lucy."

Bernard raised his eyebrows at her. "That Tom's a busy boy then," he chortled.

Fen felt herself going rigid and headed quickly for the door, protesting: "Not that, Bernard. You've got a one track mind. You know what they say about people who constantly talk about sex."

Bernard lobbed another bit of cotton wool at her departing back, laughing. "That they are stupendously good at it? See you later, poppet."

Fen fell asleep on her unmade bed as soon as she lay down; a shallow listless sleep, subconsciously still listening for the knock on the door, images of Lucy and Tom shouting at her and beating her with cotton wool flashing across her brain.

She awoke feeling slightly more resilient, knowing what she needed to do. 'First I must see Lucy, try and make things better.' She cursed herself for not having done it yesterday, for being too cowardly. And Tom, she didn't hold out much hope for making things better there, he had been so angry. She felt a little angry with him now, for making it all her fault. She brushed her hair savagely, hurting herself with the dragging of the brush. 'But you knew,' she scolded herself bitterly. 'You knew how it would end.'

She trudged slowly up the narrow wooden stairs to Lucy's attic room and knocked nervously on the door, her heart racing. Natalie opened it, and Fen could swear she saw something a little different in the way she looked at her now, as if something had changed since yesterday. But her manner was as bright and friendly as before.

"Hi Fen! Lucy's already gone up, I'm afraid. Early start this morning. I'm lucky, got the morning off."

Fen noticed she was wearing pyjamas. "Nat, I'm sorry. Did I wake you?" Natalie shook her head and smiled.

"Don't worry. It's a glorious day. I might go and sunbathe on the roof. See you later!"

Fen considered joining her up there when she had finished her morning's filming. It was a precarious climb out through the attic window, but the views were beautiful and you could lounge on the hot grey slates undisturbed for hours. She felt calmed at the thought. After she had apologised to Lucy for duping her and to Tom for her big blabbermouth, that's where she would head to, taking a jug of pink lemonade and lying there until the stars came out.

Her sandals slapped against the cool marble floor of the hall, and she caught a whiff of Tabac aftershave.

'Ted must be about,' she realised. The door to the sitting room swung open and his tall bony frame filled the opening. He ran a nervous hand over his curly grey hair.

"Could I have a word, Fen?" He stood back and gestured for her to come in. Fen felt herself go cold.

"Sit down." He pushed a pile of scripts from an old red sagging armchair, sending them flapping onto the floor.

The sunlight spread across the dusty brown wooden floorboards. Above the magnificent stone fireplace hung a portrait of a dyspeptic Edwardian lady, with three chins and an evil glint in her eye, next to a tattered child's drawing of a house with two chimneys and a cloud leaved tree. The room was littered with overflowing ashtrays and empty wine bottles. Tiny wooden children's chairs were stacked neatly all around the walls. A Dansette record player sat on what had once been a teacher's desk, next to a gramophone, whose big brass horn was pitted and stained.

Ted had his back to her, fidgeting with the knob on his walkie-talkie, trying to stop the crackling and squawking. He turned to face her, perching on the edge of the desk, hardly catching her eye. Fen sat demurely, feet crossed at the ankles, aware of the horsehair poking scratchily from the armchair into the back of her leg.

Ted cleared his throat. "You will have noticed I wasn't there for yesterday afternoon's filming."

Fen had noticed, but, in her misery, had thought nothing of it. The assistant directors often took over. She smiled and nodded, looking at him quizzically.

"Well, we had a lot of phone calls from the producers. There's been a bit of a re-jig, to do with financing and stuff..." His voice tailed off. Fen was scared now, and really badly needed the toilet. He cleared his throat again.

"Due to various reasons, not your performance I hasten to add - you've been a joy to work with."

Fen solemnly mouthed, "Thank you."

Ted stared out of the window, a muscle twitching in his jaw. "But the producers have decided that Dora must be written out." Fen gulped, her eyes filling with tears.

"Oh," she muttered softly. "I see. So I won't be back next year?"

He managed to glance at her face, then quickly looked away. "You have to go now Fen, today. A taxi has been called to take you to the station. You have to go and pack your things. I'm sorry. It's the money men...." He tailed off, abjectly.

"I understand." Her voice cracked and she gulped. She stood up, swaying slightly, and he finally looked her in the eye.

"Best you go now, Fen. Thank you for all your hard work."

She nodded, hot tears misting her vision. "Can I say goodbye?"

He shook his head firmly. "They want you to go straight away."

A hot breeze caught the door and slammed it behind her, reverberating around the cold hall. Sam was skipping down the steps whistling, a catapult hanging from his back pocket, off to take pot shots at crows.

"Morning Sis..." His voice trailed off at the sight of her, concern spreading across his freckled face.

"I've been sent home." She tried to sound breezy and matter of fact and failed dismally. "Say goodbye to everyone from me."

With the decisiveness and instinctive understanding sometimes only possible in the young, he thrust the catapult at her, kissed her cheek and hared off, his plimsolls making an ear piercing squeak on the marble as he rushed out through the grand doors, and off across the park.

CHAPTER NINETEEN

Her throat aching with unshed tears, Fen packed her belongings methodically into the blue holdall. She took a final look around the room where she had been so happy. The jam jar filled with fat white roses that Tommy had picked for her only the day before yesterday, their pretty heads drooping sadly in the heat, petals scattered across the scratched maple wood dressing table; the glorious view across the park; her pink flowered eiderdown; the chipped Victorian bath with its lion feet that the two of them had squeezed into, laughing and squabbling for space; she tried to burn it all onto her memory, so she would never forget that she had once been happy. Distraught, she shut the door behind her, closing the dream.

A taxi from the local village sat ticking over at the foot of the stone stairs. Fen recognised the driver, sitting with his elbow resting out of the open car window; he had been one of the extras in a party scene the week before, resplendent in a shiny conical hat and aggressively blowing a tooter. Ted stood at the top of the stairs looking guilty and uncomfortable. He lifted a hand bleakly and she raised one in return before bending to lift the back door handle. She had just thrown her holdall into the car when she heard a bell ringing furiously and the screech of tyres skidding on gravel. Looking up, she saw Tom arriving on his bicycle, stones flying as he leapt off, throwing it violently onto the verge.

He grabbed her hands and pulled her into him, her tears soaking his red checked shirt.

"I'll shrink your costume to dolly size," she wailed. "The wardrobe ladies will hate me too."

He stroked her hair and kissed her tear stained face. "Shush. I'm so sorry, I was horrible. Sam told me what they've done. I spent all day yesterday trying to stop this happening to you. My poor pretty Fen." She couldn't speak, clinging onto him, never wanting to let go.

Ted's walkie-talkie was squawking loudly. They could make out the words 'ran off set' and sensed Ted's increasing agitation.

"Tom, get back immediately. You are holding everyone up." Tom made a V sign in his direction and hugged Fen tighter.

"I will sort it out. We'll meet up." He shook his head angrily. "I'll finish here, then I have to go to America. Two months. Will you wait two months for me, beautiful?"

Fen nodded. She would have waited a life time. "I don't know how to contact you." She sensed him thinking fast.

"Meet me December the first, two o'clock. Oh, I don't know where. Kew Gardens. Big hot house. I'll be there. I'll wear a pineapple, you carry a copy of the News of the World."

She laughed weakly. The taxi driver had started to rev his engine and Ted was approaching down the stairs, his face like thunder. Fen slipped onto the leather seat, still gripping Tom's hand, letting go as the door closed. Tom leaned through the open window, kissed her mouth desperately and the car pulled away. She watched him through the back window, waving and blowing kisses until the drive curved and they were out through the broken down, rusty iron gates.

At the tiny red brick station, Fen looked through her purse for her money, fumbling with it as she bought a single ticket from the grumpy fat man in the office. It felt alien to her after so many weeks cloistered away. The baking heat on the platform, being away from the house and farm, made her feel shaky and agoraphobic. The train wasn't due for half an hour, so she sat under the big station clock, listening to its tick, willing the minutes away, the hours, the days, wishing it could be December.

When the train eventually pulled in, Fen was thankful to find a compartment all to herself. Heaving her bag onto the luggage rack, she opened both windows and checked her face in the mirror. 'I look like a crazy woman,' she decided, trying to flatten down her curls, licking her finger to wipe the smeared black mascara from under her eyes.

She watched the fields peppered with neat golden stacks flash by, turning to towns and roads, red roof tops and factories until the train pulled into the sleepy suburban station of her home town.

Fen's road felt crowded and small, with its neatly tended lawns and collections of fir trees, all in various colours and varied heights, standing obediently in rows.

The familiar scent of furniture polish, pastry and her father's plum pipe tobacco touched her heart as she let herself into the quiet house.

Chubby the cat mewed up to her, weaving his fat tabby body around her legs. She picked him up and buried her face in his fur.

"Have they all gone out and left you, baby? And I bet you haven't been fed for years!" She found him some Katkins in a kitchen cupboard, glooped the stinky meat into his bowl, and then took her bag up to her bedroom.

Lying on the bed clutching her battered one eyed teddy, she gazed out of the small metal window. She found the view she had seen since childhood comforting. She watched a sparrow twitter in and out of the green leaves of next door's sycamore tree while she wondered how best to play down her sudden, unannounced, reappearance.

Luckily, when her parents returned from work, they were just pleased to see her, and accepted her explanation of her character's demise with disappointment but no blame.

"Never mind, Fen. I'm sure that Egremont bloke can get you more work," her father comforted her.

'Eggy, damn. He won't be pleased. This is the first time he's made any money out of me.' Fen decided she could worry about that later; there was Steve to deal with first.

She met him the next evening in their local pub, a lively spacious place, full of people she knew. While she waited in the garden, pulling her cardigan tighter against the cool nip of approaching autumn, she trotted out her reason for being back for friends and acquaintances who all greeted her with: "Fen, you look brown. What are you doing here?" She herself had almost started to believe the lie that she had known her character might only last for one series by the time she had repeated it seven times.

Steve handed over a gin and tonic and said, "Oh, that's a shame. Still, at least you had a good time. You look very well."

'He seems on edge,' worried Fen. 'He probably knows what's coming.'

Steve took a deep breath and blurted out: "I'm really sorry, Fen, but while you were away, I developed feelings for a girl in my office, Martha. I mentioned her in my last letter."

Fen felt a bubble of relieved laughter in her chest, but composed her face.

"Did you?" She realised she hadn't even read his last letter, too busy with her love for Tom.

"I understand Steve, I wasn't very good at keeping in touch. Does she make you happy?"

He exhaled loudly and flashed her a relieved grin. "Yeah, she does, she's amazing. Not that you aren't too," he added hastily.

Fen smiled. "I am glad. Honestly. I was thinking of moving to London soon, to be nearer the work. So it's just as well really." Fen realised this had only been a germ of an idea, but now she had said it out loud, it seemed like the best plan.

At least it would mean she wouldn't have to think of excuses not to watch 'I Live On The Farm' with her parents when it aired.

Steve spent the rest of the evening extolling the virtues of his new girlfriend; her cooking, her medals for ballroom dancing. All the while, Fen yearned to tell him about Tom, but didn't dare to speak of it again, remembering what had happened with Lucy.

'What if he let it slip and a gossip columnist overheard?' she thought, her paranoia starting to kick in. 'Plus, I am the other woman, and I have no rights at all.' She knew Steve would not judge her and she longed to tell him everything, let it spill out like a fountain, but she just nodded and smiled and made the right noises, and when he asked: "How about you, Fen? Was there anyone on the shoot caught your eye?" she just shook her head and said "No."

So she found her little flat in Tottenham, decorating it with finds from junk shops and jumble sales, killing time, willing the days to hurry by.

Eggy had been noticeably cross with her, and it had been an uncomfortable meeting in his office. He had begrudgingly got her a few weeks in pantomime in Clacton, playing a villager in Jack and the Beanstalk.

She also had a day's filming in a London hospital morgue as dead Dora. She felt sick with nerves travelling there on the underground, wondering if Ted would be funny with her and if she dared ask any of the cast or crew about Tom.

But it was a different director and crew, Ted apparently in Hollywood now, and none of the cast played a part in the scene. Fen just lay on a cold stone slab with a luggage label tied to her toe and half a bucket of Kensington Gore on her face, trying, unsuccessfully, not to breathe or twitch.

She hoped she might bump into Tom when she was called to Soho to replace some of her dialogue with Geoff. But, again, nobody else from the production was there; only Maisie the receptionist, who must have been able to see something beneath her misery and nerves to have still taken a shine to her.

Every day, she would scan the gossip pages in the newspapers, scared and hopeful that she might read news of Tom and Megan, but all she found was a small picture of them together attending a film premiere, Tom handsome in black tie and Megan breathtaking in organdie. She tore it out and spent days poring over it, trying to work out how things were from their body language, driving herself nearly mad with suppositions, until she eventually had a fit of anger, ripped it into a thousand pieces and threw it down the toilet.

CHAPTER TWENTY

"Finally." Fen shivered in the cold morning air. A wet fog pushed against the windows and she made a dash from her bed to the bathroom, her teeth chattering. The boiler banged and spluttered into life and she washed quickly in the lukewarm water. She had been planning what to wear for weeks, the clothes she had finally chosen carefully the night before draped over the back of the armchair. She picked them up and pulled a face. But it was too late to change her mind; any other decent clothes lay crumpled in the ironing basket, so she dragged the black wool dress over her head, put on the black tights and pulled on her favourite pixie boots.

She made up her face carefully, her breath steaming up the mirror. Her summer tan had all gone now, just a faint line where her watch had been.

'What if he finds me pasty?' she worried. 'What if he turns up, sees me, feels sick and runs away? What if he doesn't turn up at all, or turns up with Megan?' Fen decided to make her mind a blank. It was going to be a long trek across London to get to Kew; she would concentrate on that and worry later. Squashing down a red Baker Boy hat over her curls and buttoning up her scarlet duffle coat, she set off bravely into the fog.

She could barely see the bus as it loomed towards her, and waved frantically when she thought it might drive by. Luckily, the driver saw her and laughed at her as she clambered aboard, imitating her frantic movements. She smiled politely, inwardly cursed him and climbed to the top deck. Stilling all her senses, staring vacantly at her own reflection in the window, she began what she hoped was the journey back to Tom, back to happiness.

The heat of the Palm House made her gasp as she entered, and she struggled to remove layers of her outdoor clothes. She could feel the humid air starting to ruin her carefully combed waves, springing them up into mad curls. Laughing to herself, she remembered Tom saying he would wear a pineapple, and thought: 'If anyone can find a pineapple in December, then Tom's the one.'

She found a large palm with a seat beneath it and read the label. 'Bromeliad. I shall wait here.' She settled down on the damp iron bench and started to read the News of the World, purchased specially from a shivering road side vendor, and waited. When she had finished the crossword, she allowed herself to look at her watch. It was half past two.

All her resolve of earlier started to crumble. She put the paper beside her on the bench and walked around the Palm House, ignoring all the lush foliage, trying not to catch the eye of the one elderly bespectacled man who had been there as long as she.

'Maybe he's on a promise with Tommy too.'

She pushed open the glass door, the cold slapping her in the face, making her cheeks bright red, and peered across the gardens, desperate to see his hurrying figure dashing towards her, full of smiles and apologies for his lateness. But all she could see was a gardener raking some leaves and the ghostly skeletal form of a monkey puzzle tree.

Disconsolately, she went back to the bench, smiling tightly at the old man as she passed. Her paper had gone and she heard the door bang as he scurried out of the hothouse, the corner of it hanging out of his bag.

She started to dissect a large leaf, tearing it nervously into strips, and waited.

'Am I in the wrong hothouse?' She started to panic. What if he were waiting somewhere else, sadly looking at his watch and nursing his pineapple.

'But if I go and look, he might come here and I'll miss him.' Fen started to tremble and felt tears rising. She looked at her watch again; it was nearly four o'clock.

She picked up her coat and struggled into it, knowing that the gardens would close soon, one remaining rational part of her brain telling her that even though she wished she were dead, dying alone in the night, locked in a Palm House might not be the best way to go.

'It would be in the papers though,' she argued with herself, trudging across the darkening grass to the main entrance. 'He would know that I came.'

On the bus home, she became more and more upset, torturing herself with wild possibilities. That he had been hit by a car in the fog trying to get there; that his gran had died and he couldn't come; that he had changed his mind; that he had never meant to come in the first place and had just arranged it to keep her quiet. The last two made her angry with a white hot rage, and then guilty for believing it of him, even if only for a moment. Worst was the desolate realisation that she had no idea how to contact him, or how he could find her. 'Maybe I could write him a fan letter.' Knowing that she couldn't bring herself to be able to, that he would have to be the one to find her.

She blundered blindly across the road from the bus stop and let herself in, the keys rattling and slipping as she struggled to find the key hole. On the little hall table lay a crisp, expensive, hand delivered white envelope.

'He found where I live. He came here. I missed him.' A little nugget of hope and joy started to form in her heart as she ripped it open. Through blurry eyes, she read:

Dear Fenella,

I recently received a telephone call from Mr. Roderick Plumb of Plumb Casting Associates informing me that his client, a Mr. Tom Godwin, will be unable to attend your proposed meeting on December 1st at two p.m.

Kind regards, Harriet Green, Secretary to Edgar Egremont.

Fen read it four times, searching for anything in the terse words that might tell her why, something personal. And then, slumping down onto the grubby doormat, her back against the door, the paper hanging limp and crushed from her hand, she began to sob: dry, retching animal cries that she could not stop, echoing along the dingy hallway.

Mrs. Shah, hearing her from upstairs, shuffled down and wrapped her in large motherly arms, wiping Fen's face dry with the blue hem of her sari, rocking and soothing her, taking her into the flat and making her lie down on the bed, holding her hand until she slept.

Mrs. Shah looked after Fen constantly for the next few weeks, offering tempting curries with her broken English. They looked and smelt delicious, but all food tasted like cardboard to Fen. Hoovering around her as she sat broken and frozen on the sofa, checking each morning that she had not died from crying. Telling her over and over that the boy was bad. And eventually, Fen started to function again, eternally grateful to Mrs. Shah for the unquestioning kindness. She went off to do her pantomime, allowed a fellow cast member to flirt with her, went through the motions of seeming to be happy, her heart a tiny frozen flint, intent on never feeling anything that strongly ever again, her armour thick and tightly strapped on, vowing to herself that she would never speak of her and Tom to anyone, for as long as she lived.

She managed to avoid seeing any of 'We Live on the Farm' when it was transmitted. She thanked people politely when they complimented her performance, and changed the subject adeptly if they quizzed her about the time she had had, or the other cast members.

When Tom and Megan's new film came out, she refused invites to see it. If his voice came on the wireless, she would turn it off. On seeing Bernard in Soho one lunch time, she pretended she had not noticed his cheery wave and skulked furtively down a side alley.

And when, a year later, while filming an advert for toilet tissue, a fellow actress had shown her an old piece from a gossip magazine about Tom and Megan's split, she had said, "What a shame" politely and concentrated on dispelling her rising feelings. She even coped on catching a glimpse of a photograph of Tom leaving a Hollywood hotel with someone who looked suspiciously like Lucy in the background.

But now, and she did not know why, she could sense the mortar trickling from the parapets, hear a faint grinding of stone. Her barricades had started to crumble.

CHAPTER TWENTY ONE

A sharp burning pain brought her back to the surface. Sitting upright, she searched around for the source, convinced that somebody had crept up while she dozed and burnt her with a lighted cigarette. Her paranoid theory vaporised when she spotted a fat angry wasp crawl down her arm.

"You bastard," she shouted, rubbing at the sting furiously, making it hurt even more. The voices of a couple passing by on the other side of the yew hedge paused in their conversation.

"Someone's in trouble," the man laughed and the girl joined in with a polite giggle.

Fen froze and automatically ducked down, desperate to hide under the bench. She knew those voices. The pair carried on away from her,

"Stelly, my love, you know you want to," were the last words her straining ears could catch.

Squatting disconsolately on the grass, lavender fronds batting her on the head, she nursed her throbbing elbow. Fen wondered if it were safe to get back to the studio without Tom seeing her. She looked at her watch; she was already ten minutes late. Geoff would think she was turning into Wanda.

She peeked furtively around the high hedge and spotted the retreating figures of Tom and Stella, who had nearly reached the lake.

Tom was waving his arms around and laughing. Stella, limpid in floating eau de nil, turned her lovely face to his and smiled dreamily.

Fen fought down the urge to speed across the lawns and give Stella a big push into the lake.

'No point anyway. She'd just waft up to the surface gleaming like a mermaid.' And why was Tom laughing? 'How dare he be so happy?' she thought bitterly, when she had been so very, very sad.

She raced back through the main building and across the set of an ancient roman town, hoping that she hadn't been accidentally caught in any filming, her streaking form looked out for in years to come, like an anachronistic white van in a period drama.

They all looked up as she rocketed into the studio and a smug smile played across Wanda's face at having arrived before her. Fen could feel her face burning as hot as the wasp sting.

"I'm so sorry..."

Geoff patted her kindly on the shoulder.

"Don't worry. We've only just set up. Shall we do a track of moves first? Give you both a chance to see what you're in for."

Fen settled into a plastic school chair next to Wanda, glad of the mind numbing chore ahead, dutifully rustling away with her tatty green pillowcase whenever a female character appeared, waiting for Wanda's cloth to fall silent as she dropped off to sleep. Fen felt her muscles stiffen whenever Tom's face appeared on the screen, wondering if she could introduce a nasty scratchy sound for him without anyone noticing. 'If only I had a blackboard handy, I could run my fingers down it,' she wished petulantly.

Wanda awoke with a flourish of her cloth as the projector whirred down and said, "Marvellous!" very loudly.

Over tea, they discussed what surface the floor of a post-apocalyptic underground bunker might be. Bored, Fen fought back from offering the suggestion 'cheese' as they all went round in circles, finally settling for Gary's first suggestion of concrete with a metal bucket nearby to give it, as he described, 'a space age ring.'

Wanda selected which characters she would like to be, mostly the ones that did the least running, but also Tom.

"He's a pretty lad. Such a handsome face!" she declared and Fen's stomach flipped as she thought, 'You should see the rest of him.'

At a quarter past five, Wanda swept out of the studio to glam herself up for the journey home. Fen listlessly tidied some of their stuff away until Geoff stopped her.

"Leave that, Fen, you'll put Larry out of a job! We'll have the force of the unions on our back."

Fen dropped the shoe she was holding.

"Oh I'm so sorry. I didn't realise. I'm not usually tidy at home, I just…" She stopped abruptly. 'I just don't want to leave yet in case I bump into Tom,' she admitted to herself.

183

Geoff looked concerned. "Don't worry Fen, I was only joking. Well, actually it's probably true, but no harm done. Are you okay, Fen? You seem a little distracted."

Fen shrugged. "I'm fine Geoff, a little bit in awe of all this." She gestured around the studio.

"You'll get used to it." He moved towards the door. "Come on, don't want to get locked in."

Fen tried to hide behind him as they walked down the long corridor to the car park, bobbing around suspiciously.

"So what hours do they work filming?" she asked breezily.

"It depends. Studio hours finish at five thirty. That's when the technicians are paid until."

Fen checked her watch, relieved to see that the time was five past six.

"And where is the set for 'Beyond the Universe'?"

Geoff had reached his car and was trying to balance film cans on the roof. Fen held them steady for him as he fished about in the pockets of his tweed jacket for his keys.

"On stage thirteen I think, the big one on the edge of the lot. Found them."

He jangled his keys triumphantly. Fen noticed the resin coated picture dangling from the fob, of two smiling girls in school uniform. Geoff glanced up as her as he unlocked the car door.

"Did you want to visit? It's a bit of a closed set, I'm afraid. The cast will be doing some ADR in our studio at times." He looked cross. "In fact we'll probably get kicked out for them."

He took the cans from Fen and threw them on the back seat. "Was there someone you've taken a shine to?" He winked.

Fen backed away, flustered. "Oh no! I mean, no. Just curious. I've met a couple of them...anyway." She pointed to her car, which seemed to have acquired rather a lot of bird droppings since the morning.

"That's me. See you in the morning, Geoff."

He waved cheerily and Fen set about trying to wipe off some of the mess on her windscreen with an old tissue. Having smeared it around futilely for a while, she gave up, wondering why the birds seemed to have especially selected her car to do their business on.

'I suppose it's meant to be lucky. If that's true, I shall probably win a yacht.'

She settled herself into the car seat and tried to remember how to drive. Glancing in the rear view mirror she spotted a shiny red open topped MG zipping out through the exit. Fen willed with all her might that her avian friends might choose to relieve themselves on the smiling occupants, Tom in a flashy pair of big black sunglasses, hands in brown kid driving gloves resting easily on the steering wheel.

Fen snorted with disdain. 'Driving gloves! Should by some miracle I ever speak to you again, you won't hear the last of that. Driving gloves. Ha!'

And Stella in the passenger seat, a scarf covering her lovely hair, a long pale hand on Tom's knee. Fen scolded herself. She was too far away from them to know if the last part was actually true, but she would have put money on it, even the yacht.

CHAPTER TWENTY TWO

Fen decided to affect a disguise. She had considered
dying her hair, or even shaving her head, extensive
rhinoplasty maybe. But in the end, the preferred option was
for a red and white spotted bandana tied around her head and
a pair of oversized sunglasses with orange frames.

She was greeted at the studio by Larry, who guffawed
cheerily and asked if she had been taking in washing. Having
arrived an hour early, she mooched about the props room with
him as he proudly showed off bits of wood engineered to
squeak with a twist, making polite noises at his inventiveness.

Fen knew she daren't brave the canteen or restaurant
and had made herself some nasty cheese and pickle
sandwiches the night before. They now lay curling dryly in
their cocoon of silver foil. She had had to put a big sign for
herself on her front door, knowing that she was likely to forget
about them, and had stared bleary eyed at it for some five
minutes that morning wondering what on earth it might
mean.

As the rest of the team drifted in, she good-humouredly
endured some more washerwoman jokes and they set to work.

Wanda had taken a great shine to Tom, bordering on an
unhealthy obsession.

"Geoff, darling. Is that delicious boy coming in soon? I'd
like to see him in the flesh."

Geoff buzzed through on the talkback from the control room.

"I expect so. They'll all be coming in. It will be a damn nuisance though, holding us up."

"I doubt that boy could ever be a nuisance. Look at him."

Fen noticed that everyone was being too polite to point out that Wanda was actually old enough to be Tom's mother, though she could feel herself getting close to the point, if only to stop her going on about him.

"Is he single?" Wanda was relentless.

"I have no idea."

"Is he straight?"

Fen wondered if she should pipe up that she could vouch for that. Geoff sighed.

"Well he appears very chummy with the lovely Stella by all accounts, and he was engaged to Megan Thingummy, that Hollywood stunner. Plus there are rumours of a couple of girls in between. God, you've got me gossiping like an old biddy. Just do his feet for me, will you?"

"I'd do more than that." Wanda saucily nudged Fen, whose smile felt stapled on.

A couple of girls in between? Her stomach felt liquid with misery. 'Is that all I was?' she questioned herself. 'A girl in between?'

Fen ate her sandwiches outside the back door of the studio, taking care not to plunge into the water tank as she manoeuvred a blue plastic chair out into the sunshine. She was annoyed that she had turned down the chance of a free meal in the restaurant with Wanda and Geoff. The thought of the succulent delicacies they would be tucking into made her lunch taste even more depressing. They could not understand why she wouldn't join them, her feeble excuses of special dietary requirements unconvincing, especially as they had both seen her trough her way through four courses on many occasions.

'But what would I do if Tommy and Stella came in? Fall face down in my dinner? Hide under the table? Behind the flower arrangement?'

She decided the nasty cheese was her only option, safely hidden behind the big double doors, her legs stretched out in the sun, breathing in the petrol fumes from the passing trucks.

Wanda and Geoff arrived back late and tipsy. Fen and Gary had already made a start on making the papier-mâché headed alien sound more convincing by squishing around with a melon. Geoff listened back to it and gave it the thumbs up. He looked as if his ears were on fire from Wanda's relentless lunchtime onslaught, and she wasn't intending to give up.

"That young man was in the restaurant, Fen, and that old meanie..." She jabbed her thumb in Geoff's direction, "wouldn't introduce me. Would you?"

Geoff raised his eyebrows at Gary next to him, who, when not pressing the record button, was completing the crossword in the Sun newspaper.

189

"He was deep in conversation with his beautiful co-star. I could hardly interrupt them and introduce you."

Fen sensed that Geoff had left the words 'as some mad old bat who walks about on gravel' unspoken. She wanted to know what Tom might have been telling Stella. That he would meet her later, but that she must keep it a secret? She felt the familiar constraint tightening in her throat.

"Now can we get on? Fen, carry on with your alien, it's sounding good," Geoff insisted, his patience paper thin.

Wanda went sulkily to sit in an armchair and the picture rolled.

They were making good progress through the afternoon; even Wanda seemed keen, creating a rather brilliant alien stun gun sound from a pair of Bakelite headphones and a metal tobacco tin. But then the studio lights went up suddenly and Fen felt her stomach flip, her eyes darting towards the back door, seeking escape.

Geoff's voice crackled through.

"Sorry guys. The director is here with Stella. They need to do some dialogue. Stand down for the day."

Wanda didn't need asking twice and swept out, waving cheerily. Fen, relieved that it wasn't Tom, started to pick bits of melon seed from under her fingernails in case she might be required to shake hands. She doubted very much if Stella would remember her from before, but thought it might be polite to meet the director.

As she entered the control room, she saw a familiar, tall, rangy figure standing next to Gary and caught a waft of Tabac that sent her heart spinning back through time. She stood motionless and pale in the doorway, trying to find a reverse button so she could scoot back unnoticed into the studio.

But Ted looked over, a look of guilt and embarrassment on his bony face.

"Fen. Hi."

"Hello Ted, nice to see you." She took his proffered hand and shook it.

Geoff looked from one to the other.

"So you've met? Good, good."

Fen returned Stella's vague simper.

'Not a clue who I am then,' decided Fen

"Have you been busy, Ted?" The perpetual question for the freelance worker.

Ted nodded.

"Yes, I've been very fortunate. I went to Hollywood with.., after 'Farm' wrapped, did a bit there. You? Still acting?"

"Doing some sound effects at the moment. I'm enjoying it. Anyway, take care."

She could tell that Ted wanted to say something to her, to try and make things better. She decided not to prolong his misery and made her way out, feeling the look from his sad eyes on her back. She tried to transmit her thoughts to him telepathically as she passed by. The words ran incessantly through her brain like a mantra. 'Please don't tell Tom I'm here, please don't tell Tom I'm here, please don't tell Tom I'm here...'

Resting her head on the steering wheel, she began to wonder how much more her poor nerves could stand. 'I could just meet him, say hello brightly, keep dropping the name of my imaginary boyfriend into the conversation, wish him well and no hard feelings,' she told herself.

But she knew that, if such a conversation were ever to take place, she would need to be wearing something over her face, the stinking cloth she used for moves maybe, because if he saw her eyes, they would give it all away. The loss, the terrible pain of missing him, the anger at how carelessly he had treated her, all of these still lay inside.

She started the car engine, mentally counting down the days left on the programme. Geoff had mentioned that there was only a couple more weeks filming left for the interiors, and then the cast were back to a gravel pit in Wales to do a few pick ups. If she could just keep hidden for a little longer, then she could really sort out her brain, start living her life again.

CHAPTER TWENTY THREE

"You want us to use what?" Wanda stared incredulously at Geoff, her mouth curled with distaste.

"The wet newspaper just isn't doing it for me. And Querxl is a major character in this episode. Ted was quite insistent he wanted the sound just right at the spotting session."

"Ha!" spat Wanda. "What do directors know? He won't be able to tell what we've used."

Geoff tried to remain calm. "He might if he decides to drop by and see us. Which he has suggested might be the case."

"Fen will have to do it. I'm not sticking this manicure in a fish head. Luigi's taking me to the Grosvenor tonight."

'I bet you're paying though.' Fen gazed mournfully at the giant cod's head that lay on a tarpaulin in the middle of the studio, and it gazed mournfully back.

"Are you happy to do it, Fen?"

Happy probably wasn't the word she would have used; manhandling a stinking fish head didn't appear anywhere high on her list of jolly things to do of a Thursday afternoon. She was with Wanda on this one, and wanted to show some solidarity. But it was their job, and needed doing. Querxl, lord of the fish people from the planet Splood, at present, sounded like the rustling nylon suit the actor was actually wearing.

Glad that she'd opted to wear an old grey t-shirt that morning, instead of her pink top from Biba, Fen stood up and cracked her knuckles.

"I'm going in."

The feel of it was disgusting; sharp silvery scales prickled her fingers, and she was terrified one of its eyes would pop out as she rolled it about in time to Querxl's movements. She loved Geoff, but swore that, if she heard his voice one more time saying "Good, good, bit more energy," she would batter him about the head with the cod. Too much energy and it would explode all over the studio, showering them all with brains.

'But you're alright, matey, stuck behind the glass in your leather swivel chair. You're not the one grubbing around on the floor, getting a cricked neck, with their hands in a fish. You're not the one who will stink for a month and lose all their friends...'

She couldn't help her replies to him becoming more and more terse. She had never been aware how much underlying venom you could manage to convey with a brittle "Okay!"

Sadly for Fen, Querxl, lord of Splood, was holding a reception at his embassy and had decided to do a crazy marine dance. The cod's head was heavy, and her arms were getting tired as she tried to wave it about.

Her ordeal seemed to go for an age, but eventually the end title roller started and the studio lights came on.

Fen sat back on her haunches and mouthed "sorry" to the poor battered fish head she was still holding. In fact, she wasn't sure if she was able to take her hand out of it. Its insides seemed to have moulded themselves onto her.

She started to panic slightly, looking about for someone to help pull it off. Wanda appeared to have quietly slipped away at some point, Larry was in the back room making tea and Terry had nipped out through the back doors for a smoke.

She gazed in desperation towards the control room. Gary and Geoff seemed to be preoccupied with another figure, laughing and joking, patting each other on the back. Fen tried to get up, but the tarpaulin was slippery with scales and blood, and with her hand stuck in the fish head she couldn't manage enough leverage to stand upright. She slipped miserably onto her bottom.

"Geoff!" she shouted, but they had turned off the microphone and couldn't hear her.

"I'll just sit her and stink then, shall I? You complete bastards. When you've quite finished your chat about football, golf and breasts, perhaps one of you might see fit to relieve me of this giant fish mitten you've made me wear for your poxy television programme, you complete arses."

Fen figured if they weren't listening to her, she might as well say what she really felt.

"And when, or if, I ever do get this bloody thing off of me, one of you will be wearing it as a hat."

"Fen."

She skittered around, her feet slipping away from her. Because of her heated tirade, she hadn't heard the side door open.

"You have your fist in a fish."

Fen realised her chance to skid across the studio and dive into the water tank, just holding the cod's head above her, had been and gone. She sat slumped and silvery with scales, nursing the fish on her lap. All she could manage was to open and shut her mouth a few times; it became hard to tell where the fish ended and she began. Eventually, she managed to squeak:

"In a fish, yes."

"How have you been keeping?"

"Packed in ice." Fen had meant it as a feeble fish pun, but realised it was the first real truth she had uttered for a long time.

A small tight laugh came from the shadows in the corner of the studio.

"Still funny then. I'm doing some dialogue replacement apparently. Is Ted here?"

Fen nodded towards the control room.

"Through there. You might have to wait a bit until we clear this mess away."

"Oh. That door?" Tom stepped nearer to her, out of the gloom. He was wearing a tight silver space suit, taut across his lean muscles.

'And I am wearing a fish head. In fact I am stuck in a fish head for ever.' Fen wanted to die, there and then, laid out on the tarpaulin. They would have to bury her with the cod still attached.

He walked away from her, but paused as he touched the door handle.

"Do you need a hand? I mean, instead of that fish one?"

Fen really didn't want to ask for his help, ever. But the need to escape overcame her pride.

"Yes," she bleated, and he walked towards her. As he neared, she allowed herself a brief look at his face. He looked tired. Sad.

She recoiled slightly.

"No!" She realised it may have come out more forcefully than she had intended.

"Get Geoff to help me. You'll get your space suit fishy."

He seemed hurt, but she couldn't understand why. Did he really want to pull a cod's head off her hand? 'He hadn't even wanted to turn up to tell me goodbye,' she thought bitterly. 'So he can keep his hands off my cod.'

The other men emerged from the control room and shook hands with Tom. Nobody bothered to shake head with Fen.

Geoff looked down at her, trying not to laugh.

"Poor Fen. If it's any consolation, it sounded great." Ted nodded his agreement.

"Larry!" Geoff called him from the back room, a few times as Larry was hard of hearing. Eventually, he appeared and bumbled across, pulling on a pair of rubber gauntlets that he'd picked up on route.

With a big heave, the fish head was released, making a comedy plop as it left her hand.

"Damn, we should have recorded that!" guffawed Gary.

Geoff handed her a towel.

"Go and get cleaned up best you can, Fen, and then you might as well get off home. We've got some work to do with Tom. Have you two met?"

They both mumbled "Yes" and Ted glanced from one to the other, neither of them noticing the compassion and concern in his gaze.

"You came straight from set then, Tom?"

Tom looked down at his space suit, anywhere to avoid catching Fen's eye, which was highly unlikely as she was busying herself trying to pick up her bag without touching it.

"Not my usual attire. Well, maybe on special occasions."

The men all started laughing and making ribald jokes and Fen wanted to kill them all. She tried to edge past them and out of the door, wishing it wasn't Tom that was blocking her path. Forced to say something to get him to move, she said feebly.

"Nice to see you again."

He gave a curt nod.

"Oh yes, you too Fen. See you then. Bye."

CHAPTER TWENTY FOUR

"So that's it then," Fen told her reflection in the mirror of the ladies' toilets. She noted that one of the fish's eyes had indeed popped out and was nestling in the middle of her hair. "The grand reunion, hearts and flowers, embraces in the rain, sweet words, tears and kisses. No, not for me. I get cod's heads and space suits and see you then, bye."

She scrubbed at her arms with carbolic soap, scratching them raw, hoping the pain might mask the one in her heart.

Fen had never really allowed herself to hope, not consciously. But with the disappointment she felt now, she knew that, deep down in her soul, she had been waiting for the day when she might see him again. For all the hiding and the fear, she realised it had been necessary for her.

'Maybe now it can really be over,' she prayed. 'That was how my big love affair ended. Not with a bang but a fish scale.'

Some of the worst of the smell from her hands had gone and she chucked the towel into the bin, wondering what on earth the cleaners might make of it the next morning. She checked herself for a final time in the mirror, unsurprised by the dead look in her eyes. It was in Tom's eyes too. She pondered who he might be grieving for. Maybe Stella had turned him down. Or maybe something had happened to his gran. The thought made her catch her breath sharply, shocked by the wave of concern she suddenly felt for him.

She fought back the desire to return to the studio. He would be busy; Ted, Geoff and Gary were there. No need to embarrass herself further in front of them.

'And what could I say? Sorry someone has made you feel as sad as you made me. You git. That would achieve nothing.' Dry eyed and with a heart of lead, she began her long, stinking drive home.

She lay in the bath for nearly three hours, staring at the pig shaped damp patch on the ceiling, caused when the Shah's sink had overflowed, there so long now it had become a feature. When she heaved herself out, the water sparkling with shed fish scales, her fingers looked like walnuts. She wrapped her damp hair in a towel, pulled on a dressing gown and lay on the bed.

Wide eyed, a faint waft of the sea still pervading her nostrils, she wondered what to do with the rest of her life. By the time she went in to record the next episode, he would have gone. The chances of them running into each other again were almost impossible, given that she had selected a career of dark studios and funny noises. At best, she might spot him from afar in Soho, but there were countless back streets to scurry down if that happened.

'And even if I do bump into him, it will be the same as today. Pleasantries, saying words, yet saying nothing at all.'

Fen felt a tear trickle down her cheek onto the pillow. 'Nothing is resolved. It's still over.' She started to muster some strength. She would go out more, maybe she and Maisie would bump into that handsome Frank again at the club. She would get back in touch with old friends. Not Lucy though, that was too broken. And perhaps, eventually, she would even forgive herself for being such a fool.

As she rolled over to turn out the bedside light, a thought struck her, an acknowledgment that, despite everything, she was still glad she had known him; that, deep down, while her life went on, she would nurse the memory of him in her heart, her special secret.

'And when I am old and dribbling in my rocking chair with my family about me, maybe then I might mention my lost love.' Feeling a bit nauseous at her own sentimentality, she added to herself, 'Not that he deserves it. Bastard.'

"So they've finished filming here then?" Fen double checked with Geoff.

He looked bemused. "Yes, I said. Wanda keeps asking me too. She hasn't forgiven me for not being here when that Tom Godwin came in. Can't see how it's my fault though. She was the one that sloped off with a pretend sudden emergency dental appointment, leaving you to deal with the fish." He chortled at the memory. "Poor Fen, you did look a sight. I hope you weren't harbouring a secret crush on him! I don't think he saw you at your best!" Still laughing, he returned to his seat in the control room. "Where is Wanda, by the way?"

"Ladies," Fen replied shortly, still smarting from the mental picture of herself squatting on the floor covered in fish brains and Tom resplendent in his space suit.

Geoff sighed. "That bloody woman. If she weren't occasionally brilliant, I'd sack her on the spot. Oh, and while she isn't here, I forgot to tell you, they were all over the moon about the sound for Querxl in the dub. Ted's asked if he can buy you dinner in the restaurant after work. To say thank you for putting yourself through the ignominy."

Unbeknownst to Geoff, Wanda had appeared silently behind him, her face a picture of outrage. He jumped as she barked, "What about the work I did? Why am I not invited?"

Fen ducked down behind the control room window. Geoff could deal with this one on his own.

"Wanda! I didn't see you there! Of course we all know what a magnificent input you've had into the series. It's just that Ted knows Fen from before, and what with her getting so messy..." Fen could sense his desperation now.

"Well then, I'm sure he won't mind me joining them."

Wanda came and joined Fen in the studio. Ram rod straight and imperious, she gave him a look that could wither an oak tree.

"But Wanda, I was hoping I might be able to stand you a meal in town. There's a very tricky alien race in this episode. They're made of clouds and I desperately need your input and ideas. Haven't got a clue how to give them a sound, really need your expertise." Geoff sighed inwardly, tired in advance at all the buttering up he was going to have to do..

'Cotton wool and corn flour,' Fen wanted to suggest, but wisely kept her mouth shut.

202

Wanda started to line up her shoes, each pair bearing the name of the character she used them for, written on a piece of gaffer tape.

"If I must. I might have a few ideas."

'Cotton wool and corn flour,' Fen thought again.

Wanda pulled on a hiking boot.

"I enjoyed the Grosvenor with Luigi. We had a very lovely prawn dish."

Fen could hear Geoff furtively going through his wallet.

"Of course, wherever you like. My treat."

Gary mouthed 'expenses?' and Geoff nodded.

"Let's get started then, ladies. The first cue is Branja's feet on hillside. Oh and Fen, Ted said to meet him there at six o'clock. The restaurant in the main building, on the terrace."

"You'll enjoy it dear," Wanda told her, condescendingly. "Quite nice food. Not a patch on the Grosvenor, obviously."

"Obviously," Fen smiled. She didn't really want a meal with Ted. He might want to talk about old times and she was over those now. Still, free food was free food. She decided she would just engineer any conversation so that Ted could talk about himself; no trips down memory lane allowed from now on.

"Was I Branja?" Fen asked, knowing full well that Wanda would say yes, especially since the character had developed a limp after a battle with the fish people in the previous episode.

"If you like, dear. I'll take over if it gets too tricky."

CHAPTER TWENTY FIVE

It was far grander than Fen had imagined. Gilt chairs on an opulent red carpet, glittering chandeliers, a pianist tinkling popular hits of the day in such a way as to make them barely recognisable. Grey suited producers talking money with flamboyant artistes, pretty girls selling their souls and more besides on the promise of a walk on part in a film.

None of them gave Fen any regard as she passed by. She wished she had known before that Ted would ask her to dinner. Her blue gingham shirt had a button missing and her jeans were dirty from work.

A grand looking waiter directed her out through the double glass doors. She presumed he was a waiter; he could have strayed off one of the sets for all anyone knew. He too was probably waiting to be discovered.

Fen wanted to ask if his French accent was real, or did he really hail from Bolton.

"It eez table four, Madame. Zee gentleman has already arrived."

He pointed across the sunlit terrace to the far corner. A crumbling stone urn stood beside the table, planted with a tall standard fuchsia, its flowers dangling like fat pink ballerinas, dancing in the evening breeze, purple lobelia dripping down around the edges.

Fen went over, searching for Ted's grey hair.

'He must have dyed it. Do I pretend not to notice?" The man sitting with his back to her at table four, preoccupied with staring out across the lawns, had dark brown hair, and looked younger.

He turned at the sound of Fen scraping back the chair. She paused, perched on the edge of the seat.

"I'm sorry. I think I've got the wrong table..." She made to leave.

"Table four. Did Ted invite you?" Tom asked, unsmiling.

"Yes, this must be a mistake. I'll go and find him..."

"He asked me too. You might as well sit down. You're making my knees hurt watching you hovering. I daresay he'll be here soon enough. God only knows what he thinks he's playing at. What do you want to drink?"

A waiter was by his side in seconds. Fen would have liked a glass of beer, or maybe strychnine. She decided that the former wasn't very sophisticated; after all she was meant to be changing for her new life. And the latter wouldn't be very tasty. Also, she would die a horrible, painful death in front of him, involving vomiting on his shoes. Tom was drinking a Martini.

'Pretentious knob,' she thought bitterly.

"I'll have what you're having."

"Two more dry Martinis please, Maurice."

The waiter drifted away and they sat in an uncomfortable silence until he returned with their drinks.

Fen took a sip and managed not to pull a face. Tom was twirling the olive around and around in his glass. She wanted to slap his hand to stop him.

"So!" she managed brightly, breaking the silence. "Are you enjoying making the series? I thought you were all off to a gravel pit by now."

He looked up briefly, examining her, as if she was one of his alien adversaries from the show.

"I go next week. Ted asked me to meet him here to discuss it. Why are you here? You're not getting a part in it, are you?"

Fen felt hurt at his obvious concern that this might be the case, but let it pass.

"He wanted to thank me for doing the fish noises. Are you having fun working on it?"

'As much fun as we had?' The un-asked question in her mind.

He started to fiddle with a silver napkin ring, tracing the Chivergreen crest with a long finger.

"It's good. The people are nice."

"Stella's very beautiful."

Fen could not believe she had allowed herself to say it out loud.

He gave a wry smile.

"Yes she is. And very dull. Also very persistent. Bit like your friend Lucy. Did you know Lucy followed me out to

Hollywood? Got a job on the film. Ted too, director on the second unit. Big feathers in both their caps."

Fen looked across to the high yew hedges surrounding her hidden garden.

"Me and Lucy aren't in contact any more."

"Really?" He looked surprised. "People did very well out of me." His words were quiet, resigned. He looked up. "And you. What did you go on to after?"

"I got three Hollywood blockbusters and a lead in a period drama series for the BBC on the strength of my association with you." She could not keep the anger from her voice.

"Did you?"

"Of course not, you idiot. I did a panto in Clacton, third villager in Jack and the Beanstalk. Or should I try and make it sound more impressive, say I worked on 'Stalk'? And now my agent's dropped me and I mess around with giant stinking cod's heads for a living."

Tom savagely speared the olive in his Martini with a cocktail stick.

"Don't be angry with me, Fen. It was you who got your agent to write me a shitty letter." He met her eyes properly for the first time in three years. The hurt in them shocked her and she felt a slight thawing in the tiny ice flint where her heart used to be.

"You could have at least turned up and told me to my face."

Fen's world was reeling. Surely these were her lines. Was he cleverly trying to deflect the blame onto her? She began to wonder if he was playing her again. Was this a clever game? But his eyes were telling a different story.

"I did come."

Fen spoke so quietly, so sadly, Tom wasn't sure if he had heard her correctly.

"I did come," she repeated. "I sat under a pineapple tree. A weird man stole my News of the World. I waited hours. You never came. And when I got home, there was a hand delivered letter from your agent to my agent saying you couldn't make 'our appointment'. Appointment, Tom?" She tried to stop the tears spilling, swallowing hard.

The evening shadows were lengthening. The waiter appeared noiselessly and lit the single candle between them, pausing briefly on the off chance that they might eventually order some food.

Tom looked confused.

"But I got a letter too. The day before. I'd just got off a long haul flight and there it was. I rang my agent, but he wouldn't give me a phone number. He said that that Eggy bloke told him those were your express wishes, not to contact you. You waited for me?"

Fen nodded, struggling through stifled sobs to say: "Why would they do that Tom? I don't understand."

Tom looked furious. He threw down a handful of money onto the table and pulled her out of her seat, pulling her towards him tightly.

"These bastards are beginning to stare." He scowled at a nearby actress, who had been tittering behind a menu to her companion.

"Got a good look, love? Sell it to a paper, get your name in lights." He hugged Fen closer.

"Come on, we'll go to my car."

She leant against him, faint from her mixture of emotions, distraught, yet bursting with joy to be in his arms again. He poured her into the low leather passenger seat of his MG and sat behind the wheel, pausing to tut at the driving gloves on the dashboard before hurling them into a nearby tree, where they hung limply from a branch, roosting like bats. "What have they done to us, Fen?"

CHAPTER TWENTY SIX

"I tried so hard to make them keep you on 'We Live on the Farm' Fen. I said I'd leave. I only intended to be there for the one series anyway. I told them they could keep their money, but they claimed I would be in breach of my contract and it would affect me doing the film with Megan. I'd had an advance for that, paid my gran's nursing home fees. They were going to make me pay it back. Megan's father had money in both productions. Couldn't upset him now, could they?"

Fen shifted away from his shoulder to look at his face. "Your gran?"

A pulse twitched briefly in his cheek.

"She died, Fen. On her own. I was stuck in America smiling frozenly at cameramen on a red carpet."

"I am so sorry." She touched his face and he turned to kiss the palm of her hand.

"And what I did to poor Megan too. I was told I mustn't break it off with her before the film or I'd be blacklisted for some trumped up reason. Wanted me to pretend to her that everything was fine. Her own father decided this. We were a marketable commodity as a celebrity pair, apparently. Betrayed by me and her dad. I did tell her, though, had to. Bless her, she said she would go along with the lie, pretend the engagement was still on. For me."

A worm of guilt twisted in Fen's gut.

"How is she now?"

He kissed each of her fingers in turn. "Fine. She married a man who adores her and they have a baby boy." He paused, frowning. "I could kill those blood suckers for sending those letters, scratching each other's backs in their gentlemen's clubs, manipulating our lives for their own financial gain. Who are they to decide what I do?"

Fen shook her head.

"Your agent needed to be rid of me to keep your face in the papers and Eggy's always been easily bribed, if it means getting more work for his artists. And I suppose you're not such a marketable commodity with me in tow. I'd probably trip over the red carpet and lie there with my bottom in the air while the cameras flashed around me," she said.

He laughed. "Idiot. Please promise me you'll do that. I'll do it too. But I suppose there's some truth in it, not the 'you taking a nose dive' bit. My agent's always trying to get me linked to the latest up and coming starlet, like a pimp. It seems to be Stella at the moment."

A truth dawned on Fen.

"That will be why Eggy dumped me off his books. He manages Stella. Probably got some juicy parts offered for her if she was linked to you."

Tom looked at her sadly.

"I stuffed things up for you didn't I, lovely? I'm so sorry."

"I shouldn't have told Lucy anything, should have trusted you to sort things out. I felt so bad though, the way she went on and on. Did you know she told me she loved you?"

"Hush. I understand now. I think she may have been a bit unhinged. Love me, my arse."

'Well who wouldn't?' Fen considered. Tom hit the steering wheel with his free hand.

"You thought she was your friend, you wanted to be honest with her. But she wasn't your friend, Fen. She was the one who told Ted and the producers. She wanted a perk to buy her silence, held them to ransom, said she would go to the papers. That's how she got the job on the film, and she still kept chasing me, never thought of you once."

Fen felt a weight lifting, imagined Lucy's lovely smiling face and let her go.

"But how did our agents know?"

He stroked a stray curl back from her forehead.

"I called mine from the States. I think that's when he started to get worried that they wouldn't manage to control me, that the puppet was becoming a boy. I told him I wanted you in my next film. You were meant to be part of my reason for signing up to do it. That's why."

"Or maybe it was done to keep me out of the film, my execrable acting skills. I'm not that bad am I?" She managed a shaky little laugh. "What was I going to be?"

He paused slightly and gave her a hangdog look.

"Erm, a prostitute."

She slapped him on the arm.

"Cheers. Tart with a heart?"

"You would have been magnificent."

"But how did they now about Kew Gardens, the exact day and the time?"

"Put a bit more pressure on Ted, I suspect. Remember, he was there when we arranged it. He must have overheard. Unless it was the taxi driver from the village, but I haven't seen his name on the credits of some big budget movies and television programmes. Ted was on the phone all that day to the producers. Maybe he called my agent too, when he got a moment between trying to fend me off and stop me from hitting him."

"I think us sitting embarrassed at the restaurant table, both wanting to run away, might have been his way of trying to make amends. I must remember to kiss him, next time I see him. If I can get through the clouds of Tabac."

Tom nodded.

"I think you're right. I shall kiss him too. He will like mine better."

Fen looked aghast. "He never is?"

"No, but I could turn him."

"I dare say you could." Fen paused, then blurted out: "I should have trusted you. Tried to get in touch somehow. Why on earth didn't I write you a fan letter?"

Tom smiled, a slow sweet smile, creasing the skin around his eyes.

"I wish you had. 'Dear Tom, you might not remember me. I'm the bonkers girl with the wild hair and the enormous appetite, especially fond of a pie. I never really let on much how I was feeling with words, but gave it all away in my big brown eyes. P.S Please would you autograph the dirty pants I have enclosed. S.W.A.L.K.' But why on earth should you have made the effort? I was vile to you when I found out you'd told Lucy. I got scared. I thought you might want what all the other girls had expected before I met Megan, a pretty boy to boast about, a leg over then a leg up in the film industry. I should have trusted you too. I knew in my heart that wasn't the way you are. I was an arrogant fool, terrified and worried for his career."

"And you were concerned for your gran's welfare, and Megan's feelings as well. That doesn't make you such a bad person surely? Anyway, who says I don't want a pretty boy? And, while you mention it, what makes you think you're so hot?"

Fen pinched him.

"Shall we forgive ourselves?"

Tom nodded, holding her gaze. Blue eyes that she wanted to look at forever.

"I think we might have punished ourselves enough. Do you still want me Fen? After all this nonsense?"

"There has never been one instance since the first time I laid eyes upon you that I haven't wanted you. But don't you need to be hooked up with a beautiful starlet to get the parts you want?"

"Parts!" Tom giggled childishly.

"And you are beautiful, Fen, funny, annoying and pig headed, and a bit greedy. You stop me being such a bitch, believing my own publicity. In fact, you make me a better person. And of course, on a purely shallow note, we could mention your magnificent bosom."

He kissed her for a while, then lay back in his seat, looking up at the stars now twinkling above them. He sighed, a long soft exhalation from his soul.

"I'm sick of it Fen, all the fake people. I'm done with trying to prove a point to others, to myself. I'll be in pantomime with you. You can be the back end of my horse."

"Ha! Still see yourself as the front end then! I don't want to spend night after night looking at your rear. On second thoughts, that might not be so bad... But seriously though, you can't give it up. You're too good. It would be a waste."

Tom looked pleased.

"Why thank you! A compliment. I think that's a first from you. No, I won't give it up. I shall sack Roderick Plumb Casting bastards first thing tomorrow morning. They can find another mug to leech off. I fancy doing a bit of theatre. Can you see me all Shakespearean? Do you think the world is ready yet for my Hamlet? Maybe I should just make an omelette instead. And would I be able to remember all those words? You will have to help me." He sighed loudly, pulling her closer to him.

"Who cares? I want other things too, since I met you, important things. A home. A family. A different adventure. Do you think you might like to come along with me for the ride, Fen?"

"I'm in your car, aren't I? But you know, you must be prepared to let me have a go at the wheel sometimes. And I'd better warn you, I'm an abysmal driver."

CHAPTER TWENTY SEVEN

As the tube train roared into the station, a blast of hot, dry air smacked Fen in the face. The only carriage with empty seats was the smoking one. She decided against arriving home kippered and opted to stand. Her arm soon ached from hanging onto the strap and, squashed up against the nylon shirt of a sweaty bank clerk, she took shallow breaths, her nose tingling from the acrid smell of his sweat.

Stoically enduring the crush, faintly soothed by the rocking motion of the tube, Fen thought back over her day at work. Simon had been quite chatty and Wanda had been surprisingly pleasant and mellow. Fen put this down to Ricardo, the new toy boy. Younger, prettier and richer than Luigi, he seemed to make Wanda happy. Amazingly, she had even deigned to do a bit of work when she could drag herself away from reading her gossip magazine.

Fen had enjoyed a raucous lunch with the newly wed Maisie and now she was suffering for it. The lunchtime alcohol, combined with the oppressive heat of a July day was making her head pound. The open window near to her gave no relief, just blowing in soot, making it worse.

Tumbling ungracefully from the carriage at her stop, she wondered guiltily how many passengers she might have managed to accidentally bruise with her bag of shoes. From the daggers she could feel burning on her back, she suspected quite a few.

Out on the street, under the London plane trees, the air felt cooler. She hoisted the bag onto her back, wincing at the twinge in her aching muscles. Happily breathing a long sigh of relief that it was Friday, her step quickened; she was nearly home.

As she turned onto the path, the sight of the town house with its duck egg blue door brightened her heart. Swaying white flowers from the climbing rose drooped down, dropping petals onto her head. Holding a stem gingerly aside with one hand, avoiding the thorns, she slid her key into the lock. The hallway smelled of polish, pastry and talcum powder. Stooping to stow her holdall untidily into the cupboard under the stairs, she cursed as she dislodged the vacuum cleaner, sending it rapping against her shin. Stepping back, she felt fur brush against her leg.

"Hello Stinky, I nearly trod on you." She bent stiffly to stroke a soft ginger body, the headache pulsing angrily against her temple.

"Where is everyone? What have you done with them? You didn't get impatient and eat them, did you?"

Stinky just meowed noncommittally and stalked off into the kitchen, harbouring high hopes that she might follow and open a tin.

Fen felt a breeze coming from the French doors at the end of the hallway, bringing in the scent of sweet peas and new mown grass. She stood quietly in the doorway for a few minutes, looking down the long narrow garden, high red brick walls keeping it hidden and secret.

Tom was sitting in a deckchair, shirt open to the sun and his jeans rolled up above the knee. His kicked off shoes and socks lay haphazardly by the side of the pond, a vivid green dragonfly darting above them.

He cradled Lillian in one arm, trying to feed her apple purée from the bowl balanced on his knee. They both looked over to her at once, identical flashes of blue. The fat baby girl with a mop of brown curls and her daddy's eyes held out her arms and giggled.

Tom smiled sleepily at her.

"Hello darling, how was the office today? Did you ask Sir for a raise?"

Fen sat on the dry grass in front of them and he handed Lillian over.

"Wanda did some work today. She mistakenly picked the character that did a lot of running, ha ha. Saw Maisie for lunch, she sends her love. Still keeps asking what on earth you see in me, cheeky mare. I did have a stinking headache, but I think it's going."

Tom stroked her head gently, trying to smooth away the pain.

"She should be asking that question the other way round. And what on earth does she see in Jim?"

Fen shrugged.

"Tom, Lillian seems to be wearing her pudding as a face mask."

Tom watched fondly as she gave her daughter a big kiss.

"She's all apple cheeked. Have you got one of those spare for me?"

He moved forward in the chair, making it creak alarmingly.

Fen made a mental note of the noise and wondered if she could manage to carry the deckchair to the studio on the train. Tom, guessing her thoughts, said: "No you don't. I'm going to oil it tomorrow. Anyway, I was hoping you wouldn't mind being at home for a little while. Guess who got the part!"

She flung one arm around his neck, positioning Lillian onto her hip.

"Oh well done, you clever thing. I'm so pleased!"

Tom twisted his fingers into her hair, leaning down to kiss her mouth.

"You know I will have to go away for a bit on location, don't you?" He looked so sad that Fen felt her own eyes fill with tears.

"Yes, my love. But I know that you will always come back. Me and Lillian will be here waiting for you, and Stinky too, but you can't really rely on him, he's a bit shifty."

Tom laughed.

"He's not trustworthy in the slightest. His whiskers are too close together. Are you sure you won't mind?"

Fen handed Lillian back to him and wiped her sticky purée covered hands on the grass.

"Don't be daft. It's a brilliant part and I fully intend to spend all your wages on clothes and parties while you're away."

She stood and pulled him upright from his deckchair, wrapping her arms around his waist, leaning her head onto his bare chest.

"I will always wait, Tom."

Lillian gurgled and patted them both on the head.

"Ow! I know my darling, and I will always come back. However, on a slightly less romantic note, I think our daughter has filled her nappy."

Printed in Great Britain
by Amazon